Sweet Little Memories

ABBI GLINES

#1 *NEW YORK TIMES* BESTSELLING AUTHOR

Sweet Little Memories
Copyright © 2017 by Abbi Glines

Published by
Abbi Glines
10 N Section Street
Suite 147
Fairhope, AL 36532
info@abbiglines.com

Interior Design & Formatting by:
Christine Borgford, Type A Formatting

All rights reserved. Published in the United States by Abbi Glines. This is a work of fiction. Names, characters, places and incidents either are the product of the author's imagination or are used fictitiously. Any resemblance to actual persons, living or dead, events, or locales, is entirely coincidental.

Sweet Little Memories

prologue

THE SOFT CLICK of my bedroom door closing woke me. The dark curtains and black out shades that covered my windows made it impossible to tell if it was morning or not.

Yawning, I rubbed my face hard. I couldn't have been asleep long. It felt as if I'd just gone to bed.

"We're home," Hilda whispered.

That was enough to wake me up. Grabbing the covers, I quickly sat up and squinted to see in the darkness just as I felt her sit down on the edge of my bed. She was close enough that I could smell her perfume.

"What are you doing in here?" I was panicked my father would find her in my room. He'd forgive her easily enough. It was me he'd blame and I'd pay for this.

Her hand touched my thigh and I jerked away.

"I've missed you." She sounded pouty. I could hardly see her in the darkness of the room, but I knew her expressions. I could imagine the pouty face she was making as she spoke to me. Two months ago, I would have gotten hard and excited from her presence or touching me. I knew what to expect from her. Now, her presence was different.

"You can't be in here." I spoke firmly, disregarding her responding sigh. Didn't she know she wasn't welcome? When she was working as our housecleaner, I was thrilled to have her sneak in my room and suck my dick. I liked her even better the day she stripped naked and straddled me then fucked me. And we had fucked a lot. At least until my dad had decided she was going to be wife number three.

"I've been in Spain for three weeks. Haven't you missed me?"

"Are you kidding me?" My voice conveyed the incredulousness of the situation. She was my stepmother now. Had she really thought we'd continue as we had? As soon as my father had put an engagement ring on her finger, we stopped touching each other. She had become the adoring fiancée and spent her time planning the wedding. No more blow jobs in my closet or fucking in the pool house.

Her hand found my leg again. "He's old and he's mean. I miss you. I miss your body and the way you make me feel." She leaned closer to me, forcing me to back away. I didn't have much room to avoid her touching me.

"You married him. Deal with it," I replied as coldly as I could. I understood better than anyone how mean he was. Mean was too kind a word to describe my father if you asked me. I had warned her of his anger issues. She hadn't listened.

"Winston." She sighed and leaned into me. I felt her breath on my cheek. "Don't hate me. I can't do this without you. We need each other." Her hand found my dick and it didn't stiffen immediately the way it once had at just the sight of her. The image of my dad walking in on us was enough to keep my dick limp. She had no idea how bad his anger could get.

"I need you to leave," I demanded. She didn't move away. She didn't seem to hear me at all. Her mouth found my neck and she started placing soft kisses below my ear. Frustrated, I grabbed her arms and forced her away from me. "Don't you get it? He will fucking kill me. You won't be his wife long. He has his divorce attorney on speed dial, and that prenup you signed is ironclad. This can't happen. You don't want the outcome any more than I do."

She sniffled and sounded like she was crying. I sighed in frustration as I left the bed and stomped across my room. I knew well enough where things were to maneuver in the dark. She didn't. At least I hoped she didn't.

"He works all the time. He's gone now. He dropped me off and left without an explanation. I'm all alone. I need someone to hold me."

She had flirted with him, dressed in barely any clothing when he was around and successfully reeled him in. She got what she wanted. It was time she learned what it meant to be his wife. His constant absence was part of it.

"He will rarely be home. You'll be given unlimited funds to spend. Slowly, you will grow apart, and in time, he'll replace you. You'll get a nice home, enough money to live comfortably and you can even join the ex-wives club. I hear the others have started one." That last bit was a lie. My mother and former stepmother hated each other.

"I don't care if he's here. He's not the one I want. My body craves you. I miss your touch. I miss having you inside me. I need you to make me come." I heard my sheets moving as she spoke.

I wasn't sure what she was doing and my annoyance level was breaking records. The reason for the sheets shuffling was soon unveiled. "I'm naked. Come back to bed. Fuck my mouth."

The thought of seeing Hilda naked in my bed sucking my dick had me hardening against my better judgment. I wouldn't do anything about it though. I wasn't an idiot, but I would end up getting myself off with that image once I got her out of here. Girls my age didn't suck cocks like she did. Her cock sucking ability was pretty damn perfect.

"No." That didn't sound nearly as threatening as I'd wanted to.

"I'm so wet. I've thought of you all day. Knowing I'd see you tonight. Come back here and fuck me, Winston. Make me moan."

Dammit, she had me swollen verging on painful now. I was glad I couldn't see her. That would make this worse. I knew she was my stepmother, but she still had a killer body. As good as any I'd seen watching porn. She also did dirty shit like the women did in porn. Girls my age weren't that adventurous either.

"Leave. Please get out. We are done. You're his wife, my new stepmom, and what happened before is finished."

She was silent for a moment. I listened, afraid she would stand from the bed and walk over to press her naked body against me. If she got on her knees and went for my dick with her mouth, I wasn't sure I had the strength to stop that. No man did.

"You're going to miss me. You'll want my body again. And when you do, I will be waiting. It's an adjustment. I'm here, and I understand it's different because I'm your stepmother now. But nothing else changed. I still want you."

"Then why did you marry him?" I shot back. The day she'd told me I had been devastated. Not because I loved her, but because I knew what we'd done together was over.

"You're too young. He had the ability to give me a new life. One with things I'd never had. Expensive things. Travel. It was all I had ever wanted in life—or thought it was. After the wedding, it sank in that he would never be you. He would never make me feel like you do."

Hilda was thirty. I was sixteen. Did she seriously think I believed this? How did I make her feel? Every time we were together, she was the one teaching me things.

"You married him. That's all that matters now."

We both remained silent for a while. I wondered if she'd fallen asleep naked in my bed. And if she had, I wondered how I was going to get her out of my room.

My father could never know about the time we'd spent together. Or tonight. I wasn't scared of anything in this world. I'd always been fearless. I took things as they came. I dealt with whatever life threw me. Except when it came to my father. I had been scared of him for as long as I could remember.

One day, I'd stand up to him. One day, he wouldn't control me. At least the beatings he doled out slowed down once I had grown a head taller than him. But he still beat me when he had the chance or felt lucky.

My affair with Hilda would likely get me killed. The man didn't love me. I was his only son, and his heir. That was it. Nothing more.

"Okay, I'll go. But we aren't done. I'm not giving up on you. On us."

I didn't reply. I waited until the door close behind her to breathe again. I'd arrange to leave for boarding school sooner rather than later. Staying in this house was impossible.

Chapter One
BEULAH

THE PHOTOS COULD have been Stone when he was a child. Without Jasper pointing it out, I would have seen the resemblance. Even with my heart screaming no, my head had acknowledged the truth. I knew only what Geraldine had told me about Stone's father. What I did know wasn't good. The lack of emotion Stone showed at the mention of his father was also confirmation that the man was evil.

But Stone had a son. A son that he allowed his father to raise.

"How old is he?" I asked as I heard Stone's footsteps echoed up the stairs. He'd be here any moment. I'd see him. His face. And when I looked at him, I'd see the boy.

"Six or seven. I'm not sure. I never see him," Jasper replied.

I scrutinized the last photo. It was the most recent from the pile Jasper had handed me. And I knew Stone was here now because I could feel him. He was focused on me. The current that was present whenever he was near me still prickled my skin.

"What does she have, Jasper?" His voice was hard. Cold. Threatening.

"Photos of Wills," Jasper replied. The challenge was there.

I looked up at Stone questioningly, but he was turned to Jasper. Stone's expression and body seemed to be pulsing with anger. The fury blazed brightly making it hard to inhale. Fear began to build slowly inside my chest, but I didn't move. I wasn't sure what I would do if the standoff between Jasper and Stone turned physical. How would I stop them?

"Why?" The one word was simple, but the animosity behind it made me tremble.

Jasper shifted nervously. He knew Stone better than anyone. Stone's reaction was one that Jasper had to have expected. And still, he'd walked into this building and brought the photos to me.

"She needs to know. You made sure she knew about all the lies surrounding my family and hers. It was time she knew the lies that engulf you."

Stone took a step toward him. His hands were balled tightly at his sides as the muscles in his forearms flexed in response. Veins stood out against his tan skin.

I was unable to breathe much less speak or move. It was as if I were watching this in a dream. A dream that left me without control of my body. I was a bystander watching it all unfold.

"This is it?" Stone's voice held no emotion but the rage was there. Just underneath. "This is how you choose to end it?"

Jasper didn't respond. There was silence. My eyes stayed on Stone. If he did lunge for Jasper, I wouldn't be able to stop him. I watched him with my entire body on edge in case the thin hold on his anger snapped.

Stone took another step toward him. "You didn't get what

you wanted. And this was your answer."

"It needed to end before she got hurt again." Jasper sounded defensive.

Stone's eyes narrowed, his jaw clenched and shifted as he inhaled sharply through his nose.

Jasper was handling this beyond poorly. Not that there could be a good outcome from his actions. But I should speak up. Maybe I could ask him about the boy. I needed to direct the attention to me, but I was frozen.

"I'm talking about the years of friendship. You were my family, Jasper. And this . . . this . . ." He pointed at the photos in my hand. "This is it? This is how you wanted to destroy us?"

Jasper wasn't quick with a response. It didn't matter because I couldn't take my eyes off Stone. All I could see was the pain rising through his anger as Stone glared menacingly at Jasper.

"Were you going to tell her? No, you weren't. You were going to hurt her the same way my mother did. She didn't deserve that. This was me protecting her."

"No, Jasper. This was you getting revenge like the spoiled child you still are," Stone snarled with disgust. "Leave. Leave before I throw your sorry motherfucking ass out the nearest window."

I didn't expect Jasper to leave. My body was wound as tightly as it could get preparing for the first strike. But Jasper stepped back. He turned away from Stone, but stopped in the hallway in front of the stairs.

"She knows now. That's what matters." He'd lost his smug indignation.

"Leave!" Stone's voice shook the windows.

I finally managed to tear my eyes off Stone to watch Jasper retreating. I still held the photos in my hand. As he stepped down to the top step, he glanced back at me. "You have my number."

Stone turned and lunged at Jasper as I reached out and grabbed his arm to stop him.

"Don't." I managed to say something finally. "This isn't about him."

This wasn't about Jasper. Stone felt betrayed. Although I should feel the same, my chest ached for him. Stone hadn't been the one to tell me the Van Allan secrets. He'd been the one to correct the lies. Jasper's actions were different. He'd chosen to hurt Stone. He'd sought to cause pain. Stone had no real family and he'd just lost trust in the only family he cared about.

When Stone turned to me he looked defeated. The fury was gone, replaced by sorrow. He looked hollow. I wanted to hold him. Reassure him. But the photos in my hand hadn't disappeared. The truth behind what I held still dangled out there between us.

"Is he yours?" I asked. Waiting wasn't possible. As much as I hurt for Stone at this moment, I needed him to explain. To assure me he wasn't a heartless man who allowed his son to be raised by a man who had abused him when he was a child.

"His mother was our maid. I was fifteen when my father hired her. She was young—always dressed in short skirts and tight tops. She seduced me and taught me all about sex. What happened between us wasn't love. It was simply lust. She successfully lured and married my father at the same time we were having sex. I made her stop coming to me when they were married. One month after their wedding, the morning sickness started."

He stopped speaking. He was lost in thought, his focus intense. A crease had taken up residence on his forehead—a direct result of the angry scowl on his face.

I didn't say anything. Not able to move from where I stood,

I simply waited.

"My father beat me from the time I was five years old until I towered over him at sixteen. I don't mean with a belt. When I was small, he threw me on the ground by my hair and kicked me. Held me up against the wall with his hand on my throat while I turned blue. Called me names no father should ever call a son. Broke my bones a few times, but I survived. As I grew, he threw fists at me. It didn't get less violent. I had grown, so he used more force. I was harder to hurt." He stopped and inhaled deeply before lifting his head. His expression was void of any emotion. It was an empty hole and that broke me.

"When my stepmother told me she was carrying my child, I thought my life was over. In my father's world, everything belongs to him. He always gets what he wants. If anyone tries to take something from him, his brutality has no bounds. When he found out his son had slept with his new wife before he had, my status as the son he had to abuse disappeared. In an instant, I'd become a threat. Some fucked up form of competition."

My stomach was in knots. I felt ill. I knew his father had hurt him, but I never knew the extent of the abuse. How was Stone a functioning, successful adult after that childhood? Or was he? I didn't know him that well. He'd hidden his son from me. He could be hiding more. Did he have more darkness inside that he covered up? I hated myself for thinking he was deceitful. But the fear was there. How could it not be?

"You still work for him. He's raising your son." I paused after saying that aloud. Facing it and accepting it were two different things.

Stone dipped his chin as if he needed a moment to regroup. When raised his head up he looked like a man who was silently pleading and preparing for battle at the same time. "Do you think Wills is my son?"

It was a question I had thought I knew the answer to until he asked me. I held the proof in my hand. Wasn't Wills' paternity already established? He hadn't denied anything. He had explained his relationship with his stepmother. I wasn't sure why he was asking me this now. I thought he'd explain why, try to help me understand.

I held the photos up. "Yes."

I wanted Stone to say something, but he didn't. With that one word, his entire face shuttered closed. That bored unavailable look I hated so much had returned.

He straightened and walked past me down the hallway. He didn't stop or say a word. All I heard was his bedroom door as it closed behind him.

Chapter Two
BEULAH

I WAITED, UNSURE if I was capable of staying.

After ten minutes had passed and he hadn't left his room, I decided I couldn't stay with Stone. I knew he was hurting—Jasper had cut him deeply. But he'd left me alone when we needed to talk.

My room seemed so far away now. Everything I owned was still in there although I had been sleeping in his room. I couldn't even walk to my room. I needed to leave so I could curl up in private. I had to find a way to control the complete anguish that had overcome me. Doing that here, so close to Stone, made me feel vulnerable.

I had nowhere to go, but I had a car.

My purse was still sitting on the table by the entrance. My heart was heavy as I stood weighing my options. I was fully aware if I left it could mean the end with Stone. I may never walk back inside this apartment again. The man down the hall still held my heart, even after learning his secret. It didn't matter to me if Stone had more dark secrets to unveil. I closed my eyes tightly as they burned with tears. The realization that Stone could be hiding a twisted ugly side to himself still didn't diminish my love for him. Which made me equally twisted.

Walking to the door, I picked up my purse, and left. The weight of the door closing behind me held so much significance. Despair weighed on me making it hard to leave. Each step away from him, from the happiness I'd found there, tore at my heart. What I wanted and what was right were two different things.

I stopped at the top step and looked back. Memories, so many sweet little memories were inside there. How did I leave them behind? I had to walk away and forget that my heart stayed with him. As I began to descend the stairs finally, I found a way to breathe through the sorrow. It would be a constant thing. Something that wouldn't leave me easily. If ever.

When I reached the second floor, the door was open and Fiona stood there. Her hip rested against the doorframe, her arms were crossed over her chest. She was wearing one of her running outfits. But she didn't seem to be leaving for a run. Her eyes were on me. Watching me. Sympathy was there as if she knew.

"Where are you going?" she asked me.

"I'm not sure." My car was the only place I had figured out so far.

She dropped her arms and stepped back to clear the path into her apartment. "Come inside."

Fiona's apartment was too close to Stone. I glanced up and thought for a moment that if I got far enough away my heart may hurt less. I knew that wasn't true. Nothing was going to ease this pain, but staying close to him may be easier.

It was hard to accept that he had chosen to be alone tonight when I knew he needed me.

"He may want me to leave the building." As much as that hurt to say to Fiona, I knew Stone could be very cutoff. Also, he had walked away from me. The last time I looked at his face, it was so empty. As if I had become dead to him. The memories gone. Nothing remaining.

Fiona sighed. "Who do you think called me and told me to catch you before you could leave? I wasn't standing here by accident as you were making your escape."

The small sliver of hope that coursed through me wasn't enough to ease my grief completely. But there was something. "Stone called you?" I needed confirmation.

She nodded. "Yes. He said you had nowhere to go and he didn't want you sleeping in your car. He asked me to intercept you. And if you still left and refused to stay I am to call him. He needs to know."

Because he wanted me safe. Tears welled up in my eyes again. I wanted to crumple to the floor and cry until the pain was gone or I went numb. Whatever came first.

"You coming inside before you fall apart? Because if Mack and Marty hear you out here crying they're gonna get involved. Not sure you want that."

I didn't want them involved. Explaining this to anyone else wasn't an option. Besides, it wasn't my secret to tell. Although it was a horrible one, I couldn't betray Stone by sharing it. He'd abandoned his child when he was only a child himself. The one thing that stood in the way of that being an excuse was that Stone was a man now. A successful one.

Fiona stood there watching me. Leaving might be the smartest thing for me to do. It would bring an end to this painful day. But I couldn't do it. I needed Stone to talk to me. He had to help me understand. I needed a reason to believe he was good inside. I wanted to believe that so badly. I couldn't believe he could be so heartless to his child. There had to be more.

Because of that I wouldn't leave. Stone deserved a chance to correct this. It was possible Jasper didn't know the facts.

When I began walking toward her, Fiona sighed with relief on her face.

"Thank God. I'm too tired for the drama that would have ensued had you walked out of this building."

I paused. "What do you mean?"

Fiona closed the door and turned to walk around me. "Stone would have come barreling after you like a crazed man. I don't know what's going on with the two of you. But that man sounded more desperate than I've ever heard him. No, let me be clear. I have never heard him desperate. He doesn't show emotion."

That was the man I knew. The selfless things I had seen him do. They didn't fit with the man who had a child and left him with an abusive father. I was missing a piece. I knew it. I had to be.

"Are you hungry?" she asked.

I doubted I would be eating again if anytime soon. My stomach couldn't handle food in the state it was in.

I held back the ugly face I felt like making. "No, I'm fine."

"Do you want to talk about it or be alone so you can cry and shit?"

"I think I need to be alone," I told her honestly.

She tipped her chin at me. "Thought so. Come this way."

I followed her across the living area, turning left to stop in front of a closed door. "That's the room Shay uses. It's far enough away from Chantel's room she won't hear you crying when she gets home and start asking nosey ass questions. I can appreciate you don't want to talk about it. Relieved actually. But she loves drama."

She opened the door and the room was smaller than the two I had seen in Stone's apartment. I wondered if this was what Presley's room had looked like.

"Thank you for this." I sighed as I walked inside.

"No worries. Make yourself at home. This place is laid out similar to Stone's so you can find the kitchen if you do get hungry."

I smiled my acknowledgment, and Fiona closed the door without saying anything else. I waited a moment then let my legs give out as I sank to the floor and wrapped my arms around my legs. Rocking back and forth I cried. It didn't ease the ache. Nothing but Stone could do that. The simple fact he had been worried about me only made the tears come harder.

I couldn't stop loving him. Even if he was damaged from his childhood. Even if he wasn't capable of truly loving someone. I didn't see how he could love me if he couldn't love his son. There was a disconnect that I feared would always be there.

Chapter Three
BEULAH

LOUD MUSIC WOKE me up.

When I opened my eyes, the cream-colored fluffy rug was under my cheek. I'd fallen asleep on the floor last night. Stretching, my body felt stiff and abused. Not from the hardwood floor—I'd slept on worse. My aches and pains were from the drain all my crying had caused.

Sitting up, I winced from a sharp pain in my left hip. Maybe the hard floor got a few slugs into me after all.

I sat up in the dark room and felt a blanket pooled in my lap. Someone had covered me up and turned off the lights last night.

Looking up at the ceiling, I wondered if he was home. What he was doing today? When we would talk?

The floor vibrated with noise coming from the other room along with what felt like someone jumping.

I stood up and ran my hand over my hair. Picking up the blanket, I folded it and left it on the edge of the bed.

I couldn't stay at Fiona's forever, hiding from Stone. And he couldn't ignore me forever. He had to speak to me sooner or later because I needed answers. And I felt lost without him.

Someone yelled, drawing my attention to the noise in the living room. I decided to poke my head out to see what was happening out there. I also needed to thank Fiona for letting me stay, then I planned to head upstairs because I had to get ready. Geraldine would be expecting me. A flutter of hope came at the thought of her. Geraldine would know the truth.

I opened the door and followed the sound around the corner. In the living area, I found a blonde built exactly like Fiona. She had her hair in a ponytail on top of her head. She was wearing a sports bra and a pair of tiny spandex shorts as she danced in front of what appeared to be a video game on the large screen television.

"Turn it down! I swear to God I am going to throw that shit out!" Fiona's furious voice could be heard loud and clear over the music.

The blonde didn't even acknowledge her. She kept on dancing. Apparently, I had slept through her dance off for some time because she was sweating and her cheeks were flushed. She glanced over at me and smiled, and went right back to playing the game.

"Why can't you run like normal people?" Fiona continued shouting as she walked into the room scowling. She looked past the dancing female at me. "Sorry about this." She waved her hand at the blonde. "She's a fucking fruitcake!"

I walked closer to Fiona so I could thank her and leave, but as I reached her, the blonde cut off the game.

"Done! Now stop bitching. That's more fun than running. Running is boring as hell," the girl said then wiped her sweaty forehead with a towel.

"Running doesn't wake up the fucking building at six in the morning," Fiona shot back.

The girl shrugged. "I have no time the rest of the day." She reminded me of Barbie. When she turned her attention to me she smiled. "It's nice to meet you Beulah. I'm Chantel. Sorry if I woke you."

"You woke up Satan himself with that crap. Of course you woke her," Fiona grumbled. She turned and gave me an apologetic smile. "Would you like coffee?"

"No, I need to get ready for work. But thank you for last night and letting me stay here. I really appreciate it."

Fiona reached into her back pocket, pulled out a letter and handed it to me. "Stone dropped this off."

I looked at the envelope and my hand trembled as I took it. He wasn't upstairs. He'd left me a note. I felt sick again and I wanted to run from the letter. I didn't want to open it knowing it would bring pain. Nothing good could come of this. I knew if I went back to the bedroom and curled up on the floor it wouldn't make the letter cease to exist.

"When did he leave it with you?" I asked as my voice gave away my obvious fear.

"Early, about five."

I nodded and stood there staring at the envelope. I had to open it, but doing that in front of two people I hardly knew made me feel even more vulnerable. Then again, opening it alone was terrifying. I needed Stone here. I had learned to depend on him. Even though he was causing my excruciating pain, I still wanted him to be there to help me deal with whatever the truth was.

"You can read it in the kitchen," Fiona said softly.

"That bastard better not be ending shit in a letter. That's

fucking low. I don't care who he is, that won't stand." Chantel sounded outraged.

I decided to open it and face whatever his message was with them here. Maybe if they watched over me I wouldn't fold up or shatter. I would hold it together for appearance sake. Before Stone, I had learned to be strong and trust myself. That girl was still inside me.

Sliding the letter out, I hoped they didn't notice the way my hands were shaking. He had folded it three times. I took my time unfolding it because I knew once I had, I'd be forced to read his words. Words that could destroy me. Words that I would never recover from. Words he should have said to me last night and not in a letter he left with Fiona this morning.

His handwriting was neat and small. I stared hard as it all blurred together, blinking several times until I could focus and read.

Beulah,

Spend the day with Heidi today. Geraldine has a friend visiting from Maine. She will be there for the next three days. You won't be needed while Geraldine has company.

I will be in Manhattan. Not sure when I will return. The apartment is yours to use.

Stone

That was all he wrote. There was nothing more—no answers, no promises and no I love you. He wasn't trying to keep me. He wasn't fighting like Jasper had fought when we ended. Stone was simply disappearing, and at the same time, leaving me behind.

I didn't read his words again. Instead, I folded the letter back the way it had been, slid it into the envelope and held it in my hand tightly. This was my answer. He was giving me space and time to move on. He didn't want to make me leave, but he was paving the road for me to leave on my own.

"Are you okay?" Fiona's voice snapped my attention back to the here and now. I'd forgotten they were there.

I forced a tight smile. "I'm not sure I ever will be," I replied honestly.

"Did that piece of shit break up with you in a letter?" Chantel sounded furious.

My lips started to quiver, but I pressed them together to stop that immediately. "No."

"Do you need to stay here?" Fiona asked.

"No, but thank you. I have to figure out what my next steps are. He's giving me time to do that."

"He did break up with you!" Chantel was beyond angry.

Breaking up with me would have been easier than this. At least there would have been interaction. There would have been tears. Maybe there would have been yelling. But this? This letter held no emotion. It was a cold, empty . . . the end.

Chapter Four

BEULAH

HEIDI'S SMILE WAS the first bit of warmth I'd felt since Jasper had shown up at Stone's. My chest wasn't as hollow with her beside me. She had been chatting happily about the baby blankets she was learning to crochet and how they would be making them and sending them to the "babies that were cold." A nurse who had been working in the activities room at the time told me about a homeless shelter for abused pregnant women. The blankets were for the women their small children that lived at the shelter.

Another reason I loved this place. They not only took care of Heidi but gave her things of importance to do. She loved crochet and doing something useful meant so much to her.

"I'm so proud of my new washcloths." She'd given me four since my arrival—all her favorites that she'd saved for me.

"Keep them safe. I won't be making more until after Christmas. I need to make these babies blankets." She was suddenly very serious and my heart squeezed.

"The blankets are incredibly important and needed. I know those mothers are very thankful for the blankets you make," I assured her.

She nodded her head empathically. "Those babies don't have a home. Their momma's need things. I wish I could make them clothes." She looked so sad suddenly. She had no idea she'd been an unwanted baby once upon a time. Portia had wanted for nothing and gave her baby away to a much less fortunate home. And forgotten about her. Feeling hatred for Portia would have overcome me if I didn't know Heidi had been loved fiercely by the mother she had been given to.

"May takes too long of naps," Heidi grumbled suddenly changing the subject.

"May was sick last week. She needs the extra rest," I reminded her.

Heidi shrugged then just that quickly her smile returned. "When you come tomorrow are you bringing cookies?"

I had surprised her today and told her I would be back tomorrow. She had spent five minutes jumping up and down clapping her hands. Watching her do that had helped ease my despair. She reminded me that I couldn't fall apart. Heidi was always my source of joy. She would never fully understand that. More than once she had saved me from my sorrow. Losing our mother had been the hardest point in my life, but having Heidi helped me make it through each day after.

Facing life without Stone was a different kind of pain, but just as powerful. Heidi would save me once again as evidenced by our time together today. I leaned over and pulled her into my arms tightly to hug her. It was the only way I could express how much I loved her. She squeezed me back enthusiastically.

"I love you." I fought back the tears in my eyes.

"I love you too." She pulled back and beamed her bright smile at me. "Remember when Momma made us the pancakes with the candy?"

Momma would make us pancakes with sprinkles in them for special occasions. I enjoyed the happiness that memories of Mom brought to her face. "And she would put whip cream on top if we had been extra good," I added.

Heidi's eyes widened as if she had forgotten. I wondered how much she forgot. I needed to talk about Momma with her more. The little things like pancakes with sprinkles and whipped cream. The moments Momma would want her to remember.

"Yes," she said in awe. "And one time we had choc-co-late." She had a hard time with the last word.

"Yes, chocolate syrup. We had both made all A's on our report card. It was a very good day."

"I want candy pancakes with choc-co-late and whip cream." Heidi looked wistful.

I wanted them too. From Momma's kitchen while she stood there singing at the stove. It was a wonderful scene to remember, but we would have to settle for the memory.

"I will see what I can do." I'd make us pancakes exactly how we had them.

"Make some for May too. She's never had them. I told her 'bout them."

I always made enough for May, but Heidi needed to remind me. She never wanted May left out. I didn't have a friend like that. Knowing Heidi had such a dear friend made it easier to leave her here. Momma had told me when we turned eighteen that Heidi would need her own life one day and I would need mine. She stressed to me that I couldn't look after her forever. She wanted me to chase my dreams.

I didn't know what those dreams were. Dreaming of a different life seemed so foreign now. I wish she was here to talk to or hold me.

"Let's swing!" Heidi said jumping up from our seat at the craft table.

"Let's." I stood to follow her outside to the large yard set up for outdoor activities.

On our way to the door, May walked into the craft room and Heidi ran to hug her as if she hadn't seen her in weeks instead of a few hours. May smiled shyly at me and they held hands as we continued outside. This world was easy and safe. Heidi and May were happy here and didn't experience anything ugly from the outside world. That reassurance helped me sleep at night.

We were almost to the swings when I noticed Jasper waiting by the tree nearby. The facility had security where you checked in with ID and a code. Jasper had joined me for a previous visit. I had cleared his name through the office for visiting Heidi. That was something I didn't think to change until now.

He didn't belong here. If he had wanted to talk to me he could have found me somewhere else. Not here in front of my sister.

"There's your friend!" May said pointing at him.

"That's her boyfriend." Heidi giggled as they both watched Jasper.

I hadn't explained or brought up Jasper since I left Portia's home. It wasn't something Heidi would understand.

"You two head to the swings. I will be right there." They whispered and giggled more as they ran to the swings. In their minds, I wanted to be alone with my boyfriend.

The long strides I took walking toward him were purposeful. My expression was fierce. He needed to understand this wasn't acceptable. I didn't need this right now. He'd done enough. Why wasn't he in Manhattan where he was supposed to be living now? He had been leaving Savannah. He needed to do it. And stay there.

Chapter Five

"I'M NOT HERE to see or upset Heidi," were the first words out of his mouth when I reached him.

"Why are you here?" I asked him even though I just wanted him to leave.

He shifted on his feet. "I was worried about you and needed to make sure you were okay. I know what you're going through is all my fault."

He sounded sincere, but I didn't care. "My personal issues are not things I plan to discuss here. Heidi is right over there swinging and this is my time with her. You don't belong here."

He sighed and put his hands in his front jean pockets. "I'm sorry. I just needed to see you . . . Make sure you were okay. I can't go back to Stone's and I know you're still staying there. I thought you would leave after what I showed you last night, but he must have been convincing." The tone in his voice was almost acidic. That didn't sit well with me.

"Please leave," I said. "I need to get back to Heidi."

"I'm sorry. I didn't tell you to hurt you. But I know Stone. I know his darkness and what he's capable of . . . What he will eventually do to you. I was worried about you."

Maybe his sudden appearance and words were honest. There could be more I didn't know about Stone, but that didn't matter now. Stone left me. It was over.

"Goodbye, Jasper." I turned to walk away.

"I'm always there if you need me," he called out. I didn't turn around. There was a small part of me that felt something for Jasper. It wasn't love, but we had a connection once. I had thought I was in love with him. I believed in a fairytale then. Jasper had been someone else to me—he had been a hero. I never saw his flaws. I'd been too blinded by his shine to see the tarnish. I had to remember that we all tarnished eventually—Stone included.

Heidi was clapping happily when I rejoined them. "May did a cartwheel." Her elation was welcome and blinding. "She's been trying for weeks. Practice, practice, Ms. Tracey had said. It worked." The pure joy for her friend's accomplishment reminded me that there was a perfect untarnished soul after all—Heidi's.

Later that evening, after spending all day with Heidi, I walked into Stone's empty apartment. I'd been torn about returning because it was obvious he didn't want to see me. He wasn't in his apartment now and my things were still in the extra bedroom. I thought about staying until he returned to face him. I wondered if he would talk to me and maybe even fight for us after he had time to think.

Or I could save my heart from breaking further, pack up and move. I could find a small studio apartment just outside of town where the rent was cheaper. If Geraldine wanted me to continue working for her I would. Geraldine would be a constant reminder of Stone and that be painful. But over time I should heal enough to survive him.

There was a good chance Geraldine would want me to leave. She adored Stone. If she had to choose between us she would choose him and I expected that. I wanted her to—she was all he had.

I switched on the light and let the loneliness of the empty apartment sink into me. My happiest moments had happened here. Our laughter had echoed through the halls. So had my cries of pleasure. Stone was everything I could have ever wanted in a man. It was painful to think that as quickly as I found love, it was snatched away. My relationships were cursed. Having my heart broken would never happen again because I'd never get close to another man.

I hadn't eaten anything but half of a turkey sandwich for lunch. Going into Stone's kitchen seemed wrong now. I didn't feel welcomed much less that I could eat his food. My appetite left when Stone walked away from me anyway.

I walked down the hall and into the room he'd given me to use. To get my mind off of things, I went about my evening routine of undressing, bathing, and then going to bed. I laid there staring at the ceiling making plans for the next day. I decided that after visiting Heidi tomorrow, I'd look for a new place to stay. Living in Stone's apartment without him here would be too painful. The ache in my chest grew unbearable as the silence surrounded me.

When I finally closed my eyes, the doorbell rang through the apartment causing me to almost fall out of bed from the startling unexpected sound. Untangling myself from the covers I finally managed to get my feet on the floor and went to see who was at the door. I had gone to bed early but it still seemed late for visitors. I could care less that I was wearing my pink threadbare pajamas. I doubted I would open the door anyway.

The peep hole was taller than me and I had to stand on my toes to see who was there.

Shay stood outside with a box in one hand and a bag in the other. There was someone behind her, but I couldn't see who. Stepping back, I unbolted the door and opened it.

"I was about to start beating on the door. What took you so long?" She said as she brushed past me and walked inside.

"Are you good with this?" Chantel watched Shay sashay in but stayed at the door. The worried frown on her forehead didn't cause a wrinkle. Either she had amazing skin or she had already started Botox injections.

"Doesn't matter if she is or isn't. I'm not leaving. I have donuts, some fancy ass macarons, and a bag full of tiny sandwiches that rich bitches eat with their tea. We're eating all this shit, drinking Stone's whiskey, and talking about the bastards in this world."

I turned back to Shay and she held up the items in her hand. "Might as well accept this. It's happening," she told me.

I wasn't hungry, but this was a good distraction. I wouldn't be alone and the apartment wouldn't echo in the silence.

"Come on in," I said to Chantel as I stepped back so she could enter.

"Chantel won't eat the food. Does Stone have carrots and water?" Shay's tone was sarcastic so I didn't respond. Instead, I caught Chantel rolling her eyes.

"I'll take some vodka if he has that."

"And her skinny ass will be drunk after one shot," Shay added. "Now, when is the dumb bastard coming back?"

I didn't have to ask who the dumb bastard was. However, I didn't like the title bastard being attached to Stone's name. I didn't correct her because I realized it was just how Shay spoke.

"He didn't say. But I'm not staying around to find out." There, I told someone. My leaving was real now and not just in my thoughts.

"Damn," Chantel said.

Shay dropped the bag in her hand and then opened the box to pull out a donut. She held it in front of my mouth. "Open," she commanded. For fear she'd shove it on my face if I didn't, I opened my mouth and she inserted it. "Now eat."

She walked toward the living area after picking up the bag of sandwiches. "Chantel, get the alcohol," Shay called out.

"What do you drink?" Chantel asked me.

I shook my head and took the donut out of my mouth. "I don't want to drink."

"I don't care! You are drinking," Shay replied loudly.

Chantel shrugged. "You might as well pick your poison or she will."

I honestly didn't know what I wanted to drink. I wasn't hungry. The donut in my hand didn't interesting me.

"I don't know." My reluctance to drink was making this hard that it had to be.

Chantel gave me a brief nod. "I'll pick it. Sit and eat."

I watched as she perused Stone's bar. I couldn't help but worry about them using his things, but they seemed at home here. Letting them inside might have been a mistake. Stone didn't want me here much less other people. I didn't think it was possible to get Shay to leave though. She was determined. The best thing I could do was drink, eat, fulfilling her request quickly so she'd leave.

Taking a bite of the donut, I followed Shay into the other room.

Chapter Six

CHANTEL WALKED INTO the room carrying bottles of Grey Goose, Makers Mark, and club soda. She sat them on the table and went back for the glasses. I stood there watching as Shay opened the boxes, and taking out a chocolate pastry and she began eating. "Sit. Relax, bitch. Don't stand there nervous, he's not here. This is what he gets for running off."

Shay sank into the sofa and propped her feet up on the coffee table. Stone's furniture was expensive. Sitting on it made me uncomfortable. But there was no asking her to remove her feet from the furniture—she was doing what she wanted.

When Chantel returned with glasses and ice, Shay pointed at the vodka. "Fix her something please. She's so uptight she can't sit."

I slowly bent my knees and sat on the rug beneath me. I couldn't bring myself to drink and eat on his furniture.

Shay rolled her eyes at me and Chantel handed me a vodka soda. "Drink up," she said cheerily.

I wrapped my hands around the cold glass and I looked at it for only a second before taking a long swig. Shay was right. I was uptight and needed to relax.

Shay clapped. "Bravo! Now eat a sandwich or ten. They're tiny as hell." Shay glanced over at Chantel. "You could use ten or so sandwiches yourself."

Chantel plopped on the sofa and curled her legs underneath her. It was impressive considering she had legs as long as most people were tall. "I'm drinking my calories," she replied. "Did you get in touch with Fiona? Is she coming?"

Shay reached for the bottle of Makers Mark and poured a glass neat for herself. "She's on a date. New guy."

"Ah, Bruno. I forgot about that," Chantel said thoughtfully.

"His name is Bruno?" Shay sounded amused. I had to agree the name was interesting.

"Yep. He's a school teacher. High school algebra. She met him getting coffee."

I couldn't imagine Fiona with a teacher. She seemed too glamourous, but the juxtaposition made me smile. Or it was the vodka making me smile. The bite of donut was not soaking up the little bit of vodka I had consumed. I leaned back against the sofa and pulled my knees up, resting my drink on my right knee while I ate the rest of my donut with my left hand.

"Jasper showed up, there was yelling, you ended up being intercepted by Fiona at Stone's request, Stone left you a letter the following morning, now he's gone and you're here. That's the summary I got. Want to talk about it?" Shay stuffed a tiny sandwich in her mouth.

I thought for a moment then tilted my head. "No. I would rather forget."

"Fair enough," Chantel said. "Let's talk about what you're planning to do next."

Talking that through wasn't a bad idea. I had no one else to talk and needed to figure things out. I sipped more of my drink and licked the sugar from my finger left by the donut before responding. "I think I'll find an apartment outside of town. Rent is more affordable there. If I don't keep my job with Geraldine I will have to find work somewhere else. I've been putting money away so I should be good for a few weeks."

Chantel sighed. "Damn. I was hoping you'd stay and fight with him. He needs to have a fucking reaction to something instead of not giving a shit. I get so tired of that bored expression of his."

"He's been good to me and helped me when I was completely lost. I don't know why he left really. Unless I was asking for explanations for more than he wanted to tell me. In the end, it was his choice. Regardless, I can't stay here and force him to stay away."

"I don't see why not. We like you better." Shay smiled at me while she chewed the sandwich she just popped into her mouth.

They didn't really know Stone. My assumption is that no one did—not even me. He was hard to get close to, but no matter what mistakes he'd made I knew there was goodness in him. Even if he had some twisted issues resulting from an abusive childhood. I had seen him be kind when he didn't have to.

"You haven't seen him with Geraldine. I can't describe the way he takes care of her and he's always there when she needs him. I know he loves Geraldine. He also went out of his way to help Jasper when I know Jasper didn't actually deserve it. Stone's got a good heart. He's just careful with people. There's a lot of hurt and damage inside him."

Chantel poured herself more vodka. "He's an idiot. You

see all that when no one else can see past the elitist uninterested expression he always wears on his gorgeous face. He should have kept you. He needed to keep you. All the other women in his life were with him for this," she held her hands out as if the room was why they were with him for his living room. "All the shit he has. His money. His name. And of course, his talent in the sack." She winced and gave me a sad smile. "Sorry. But I've heard the talk."

Shay snorted. "Sure you have."

I didn't want to know if Chantel had been with Stone sexually. That was the last thing I needed to picture. Her perfect body was intimidating. "Don't be a bitch," Chantel said to Shay.

Shay shut up and I was relieved. Then I drank some more. My body began to feel loose and warm as the liquid started working its magic. I laid my head back on the sofa behind me and sighed.

"He is rather amazing. I didn't have much experience with sex before him but even I knew that wasn't normal. It was earth shattering." My tongue had started wagging of its own free will apparently. I didn't care. It was true.

"And the vodka has taken effect just that quickly. Give her another donut." Shay laughed.

Before I could say anything else, a donut was in my hand. I didn't even look at it as I stuffed a bite in my mouth and chewed, smiling. The donuts were good. Calories and Chantel's perfect butt didn't seem important anymore. I'd rather eat the sugary goodness than have her body. At least right now I would. Tomorrow morning, I would likely feel differently. That thought made me laugh.

Opening my eyes, I studied the chandelier's twinkling lights above us. It probably cost more money than I had made in my short life. It was beautiful. Elegant. "Do you think Stone has ever studied that chandelier before? Like really appreciated how pretty it is when the lights are on and all the crystals glitter from the light."

"Uh, no. Unless he has been sitting where you are drunk off his ass," Shay replied.

"It really is something. Do y'all think Marty and Fiona will ever hook up again?" Chantel changed the subject and I turned my head to look up at her on the sofa. She was fixated on the chandelier lights now.

"I think they still fuck regularly," Shay replied.

Chantel gasped. "Really?"

"Yup."

"I guess my asking him out is a bad idea then." She sounded disappointed.

Shay shrugged. "Not my business."

We all sat in silence for a few minutes. My thoughts were on Stone. Chantel's were on Marty and I wasn't sure who Shay was thinking about. I drank more and with each sip felt life become easier. Like I was floating on a happy cloud.

"I keep having sex with Mack," Shay blurted out.

I couldn't say I was surprised by this. "Good." My response was heartfelt even though it might not have sounded that way.

"Everyone already knows that," was Chantel's response.

"Damn," Shay muttered.

I started giggling. Chantel joined me and Shay laughed out loud with the two of us. Our laughter got louder as the world became hilarious suddenly. The more we saw each other laugh the funnier it seemed. My side hurt from laughing. Tears were rolling down my face and I was okay—at least for now. I would have face the pain again. But tonight, it felt great to laugh in the face of everything that had happened.

Chapter Seven

BEULAH

I WOKE UP to misery, but it wasn't the kind I had expected. My hands gripped the edge of the toilet as I heaved for the third time. A cold sweat covered my body. I sank down onto my knees and dropped my head into my hands once I was finished. I would never drink alcohol again.

Laughter coming from outside the door couldn't even get my attention. I didn't want to move. My head was pounding so badly that if I did move I'd likely end up hanging my head over the toilet again.

"Lightweight, you should have eaten more." Shay's all too chipper voice was annoying. How was she not hanging over her toilet? She drank more than the three of us combined. I would ask her if I could speak and not revive my nausea. But even that was difficult. "Here," a cold wet washcloth appeared in front of me. "Use that and spread out on the cold marble floor. I'll bring you some water."

I took the cloth and covered my face, curling up on the floor like she suggested. This was like a terrible stomach virus. However, I'd caused it. At least with a stomach virus you were an innocent victim. It was impossible to feel sorry for myself when the horrid state I was in was my fault.

I couldn't remember what Stone's living room looked like or how much of his alcohol we drank. When I could move again I needed to clean up and restock his bar. Leaving here was inevitable, but I wouldn't leave without making sure it was just as he left it. The ache in my chest was there under all the awful sickness. Now it was just worse. I was sick and broken. Feeling broken only was definitely easier.

"Ouch, you look worse than me," Chantel said. "And I thought I was in bad shape." I tried to tilt my head back to look up at her, but even that was too much movement. I grunted instead.

"It was fun. Worth the pain. Might not feel like it right now, but you'll appreciate it once you are up and living again. I've got to go workout. See you later."

I attempted to nod and listened as her footsteps faded. The idea of her morning workout made me want to throw up again. How could she do anything physical after last night? I must have drunk more than she did.

Footsteps approached. Shay called out to Chantel about taking the trash with her.

"Sit up and drink this." Shay squatted beside me and handed over a glass of water.

"I can't," I moaned.

"You need water to feel better. Come on you can do this."

I disagreed. I know I couldn't stay on the bathroom floor all day either. I had to get up and move on with my life. That was the one thing we all agreed on last night. It was also one of the last things I remembered clearly. No, the three of us dancing on the balcony was the last thing I remembered. Groaning loudly, I got on all fours and managed to shift into a sitting position.

"You remind me of a zombie on *The Walking Dead*," Shay said laughing.

I felt like a zombie too. Reaching for the glass of water I took a small sip. And another. I had to closing my eyes to ease the pounding in my head.

"Why?" I asked. "Why did I do this?"

"Because it was fun. And for a small window of time you forgot. You laughed and danced. We worked out your plans for the future. Although I'm rethinking the move to Spain to nanny for a wealthy widower. That sounded good when we were drinking, but now not so much. Language barrier could be your first problem."

I had forgotten that conversation. "Why did we pick Spain?" I asked wincing from the sound of my voice.

"I think you said the men there were better looking than French men. I had suggested France."

"Oh." That must have made sense last night—not so much now.

"I can show you the apartment complex where I lived for a year. It is affordable and you'll feel safe there." I vaguely remembered Shay mentioning her previous apartment last night.

"I need to clean up here and restock the bar. You can show me the complex afterward if you are available then." I drank more attempting to get myself together. An all-day hangover was not an option.

"Our party arena is already cleaned up. We can buy replacement alcohol while we're out."

"Okay," I nodded. "Thanks for cleaning up."

She shrugged. "It was my idea to drink and eat here. I'm heading to my apartment to take a shower and get dressed. If you feel like eating, I left you snacks in the kitchen. We didn't eat everything last night. Eat something, you'll feel better."

I wasn't sure I believed that but I nodded. Wait. Heidi. I'd forgotten. I was supposed to bring her cupcakes today. Due to my hangover from hell I was already late getting going today. And I was running out of time.

"I have to get cupcakes for my sister. I need to do that first." It took all my strength, but I stood up. I had too much to do and I needed to snap out of it fast.

"There are enough pastries and crap left over in the kitchen. You want to take that to her?"

I dismissed her suggestion. "No. She wants cupcakes. I'll just buy some. I don't have time to make them." I shuffled out of the bathroom and made my way to the kitchen to force a sandwich down my throat in hopes it would magically cure me.

Before I reached the kitchen, the front door opened and I froze. I knew before I looked back toward the entrance that it was him. I didn't expect him back so soon. Our awkwardness with Shay here to witness was the last thing I wanted to face this morning.

When I turned finally, our eyes locked. Seeing him so soon hurt, but it also made me warm when all I had felt was cold without him. Seeing him made it easier to breathe.

"Are you sick?" He studied me closely.

"Nope. Hungover thanks to me." Shay waltzed down the hallway toward him.

Stone barely glanced at Shay before returning his focus on me. "Where did you go?"

"Chill. Jesus," Shay drawled. "I didn't take her out partying. We drank right here in your humble abode. It should be noted she was forced. I had to call in an assist from Chantel to talk her into it. She wouldn't even sit on your damn furniture to eat until she was too smashed to remember."

Stone looked relieved instead of angry.

"I'll leave you two alone. Looks like you have shit you need to say." Shay stood in front of him and put one hand on her hip. "I think you're a bastard. Just so you know."

I paled. I didn't like her calling him that, but I never imagined she would say it to his face. "And I owe you a bottle of Makers Mark and Goose." On that last note, she walked out.

After the door closed behind Shay, Stone didn't move. He was watching me and didn't say a word.

"I was going to get dressed and move my things out today. I didn't know you'd be back."

"We need to talk," he replied.

Yes, we needed to talk. We needed to talk the other night when he walked away without a word.

My throat and mouth were frozen. I had no response. I could only stand there waiting for him to say more.

"Where did you plan to go?" He sounded stoic.

My new home wasn't his business. I wanted to shrug and walk away, but I also wanted to stay close to him a little longer. I wanted to absorb every detail of his face, memorize him.

He sighed when I said nothing. I fought the urge to tell him my plans and stood my ground.

I realized Stone was a mystery and that I would never really know him. It didn't stop me from fearing he'd always be in my head, my heart, and my soul.

Chapter Eight
BEULAH

"**D**O YOU TRUST me?"

His question sounded simple and immensely complicated at the same time. He had secrets. There was so much he kept hidden. How could I trust him when wouldn't share all of himself?

His eyes reflected his sincerity and pain. He was pleading with me.

At that moment, I realized I trusted him fully. Maybe giving him my trust was stupid or naïve. Even if Wills was his son, I knew there was a reason he allowed his father to raise him. Stone was always responsible when he wasn't required to be.

"Yes." My voice was confident and held no doubt. Admitting I trusted him allowed me to let go of my fears. I wasn't afraid of any of the darkness that lurked inside him. And I knew without a doubt that Stone wasn't like his father.

Stone's rigid body relaxed and he sighed. His steely gaze

locked on me with intensity. "I should have asked you that before. I needed time to think after seeing the accusation in your eyes . . . it was difficult for me to handle. Having some space helped me see I didn't give you a chance. I assumed you believed Jasper's word over mine. That . . . Well, that fucking killed me."

I had never seen Stone completely vulnerable until that moment. He wasn't hiding his emotion behind his hard façade. He was letting me see it all. I moved, unable to keep my distance. I walking right into his arms and we stood like that while silent tears ran down my cheeks. His warmth, security, and scent made all the pain from the past two days vanish. Without knowing the entire story, I knew I loved him. I would love him no matter the cost. That was powerful. Nothing had ever owned me that way.

"I don't know if Wills is my son," he said quietly as his chin rested on my head and his arms held me against his chest. His heart was beating rapidly.

I held on tighter giving him my reassurance as he talked.

"I was sixteen when he was born. Underage. Gilda was married to my dad. Legally that made the child she was carrying his. Without a paternity test, there was no question. I begged her." He paused and his shoulders tensed. "I fucking pleaded with her to allow a paternity test. She refused claiming the boy wasn't mine. We'd used condoms. There had been a condom break once and the timing lined up too closely. I knew if I told my father there was a good chance he'd send her to get a quiet abortion. If he thought for a second that the child wasn't his, Hilda would likely face a severe beating and then it would be my turn. I wasn't worried about what he would do to me. I didn't trust him not to force her to get an abortion. I couldn't tell him. I had no power or leverage in the situation."

My chest felt like it was going to explode from the pain that dripped from his words, knowing the fear he had felt, the unknown he now lived with. Having a child and not know if it's yours was pain I couldn't begin to imagine.

"The day I turned eighteen, I went to Hilda again. I begged her to have a paternity test on Wills. She refused. The older he got, I saw my face when I looked at him. Not my father. Me. He has my eyes—my mother's eyes. The next year, he divorced Hilda and married a model he had met at a charity event. She was twenty-two. The prenup had covered children. Wills would stay with my father. Hilda tried to fight him, but he made her life hell. She got scared from his threats and left Wills there. With my father . . . the monster. I began searching for a lawyer that was powerful enough and not scared of my father. I've finally found one. We are slowly working through how to handle this. I don't want Wills hurt by my father. I have to find out if he is mine carefully. Which is what I am currently doing." He paused, lost in thought. "I've told no one about my plight to know Wills' paternity. Not even Jasper. You are the only person that knows. The answer is yes, Beulah, I have secrets. Fucking nightmares that I kept to myself. Because it wasn't the right time to tell you I might be in a court battle soon that will make the news. My face will be all over the media if this continues. Nothing will be a secret anymore."

My hands were fisted in his shirt as I'd listened to his story. The horror of what he'd lived broke my heart. I wanted to hold him until it all went away. There was no way I could help him. He was facing something that no man should ever face. If Wills was his son, he'd have more pain knowing he'd missed all that time.

"Even if Wills is my brother, living with that man isn't a life I want for him. I've loved him from the moment I met him. Hilda was resting when she got home from the hospital. I went to the nursery and held him. I realized that regardless of who his real father was, he was my blood. My family. And I wanted him safe from the man who had made my childhood a living hell." His hands moved to my arms and he gently pushed me away from him so he could see my face. "I have to fight for him. It may be years of a court battle that consumes my time. I'll have to be in New York more and more." He leaned closer to me. "You weren't supposed to happen. I never thought that we would be here, but we are. I brought you into my life. You own me. That doesn't mean I won't fight for Wills. I can't let that go now. But I also know I can't expect you to stay with me through this. You have Heidi and she needs you close by. It's a lot to take in. I don't need an answer now. We have time."

I had somehow lost track of this conversation. He suddenly made no sense. "What answer?" I asked.

He brushed his thumb over my cheek. "If you want to continue this with me. Knowing soon my life will become complete chaos."

I didn't need time to think about that. "Do you honestly think that I would need to take time to decide to stay with you?" I asked incredulously. "There is no question, Stone. I love you. I admire your perseverance to fight for Wills. And I will be here through it all. When you need to vent, scream, or sit in complete silence. I'm not going anywhere. That's not what love is."

His shoulders rose and fell with a deep breath. "Thank God," he whispered. Then his hands cupped my face and he kissed me. The kiss wasn't wild and crazed, it was one of relief and tenderness. I pressed closer to him wanting to comfort him any way I could. If I could take it all away from him I would.

He'd been betrayed from those that were supposed to love him since birth. His father, mother, and now Jasper. Knowing Jasper had so openly accused Stone of something he wasn't sure of to hurt him turned my stomach. Jasper was a disappointment. He wasn't the man I thought he was. What he had done to Stone was very Portia-like and that made me sad. He'd been more affected by his parents than he realized. And I had been so swept away by his good looks and prince charming ways that I missed all of that.

My thoughts went to Stone. Was I missing something that also dwelled deep inside him? If so, I would accept it. I had no choice. My heart was his.

Chapter Nine
STONE

I EASED OUT of bed where Beulah lay sound asleep. She hadn't moved in over an hour. My eyes had remained open and staring at the ceiling. Not wanting to wake her with my restlessness, I decided to get up was the best idea. Holding her after our lovemaking had been reassuring. She wasn't gone. She wasn't leaving me.

Telling her the truth had been hard. It was a secret I'd held close for so long that sharing it with someone was a huge step for me. I'd debated telling her, knowing deep down she'd stay with me no matter what. I had also known I could trust her. Even if she chose to leave me she'd never share my secret.

For the first time in my life I had someone who was there for me. Someone I could lean on, share things with, and know they were by my side. The moment I saw the doubt in her eyes, I cracked. I couldn't handle that she trusted Jasper. I had to get away so I could work through it without her there, tearing me apart with her pleading eyes.

I never told Jasper about Hilda. He had been there when Hilda acted inappropriately around me though. Once he had asked if I was banging my stepmom. I'd scowled at him in disgust. The moment she'd become my stepmother it was over. Not that she didn't try to change that.

After Wills was born she got worse. When he was only four months old, she came looking for Jasper and me downstairs. Wearing nothing, she had made it very clear that she wanted us both. At the same time. Jasper's eyes had bugged out of his head. He'd played with her tits that were still massive from the milk. My father required she nurse Wills for at least six months. She hadn't wanted to. That didn't stop her from showing me her swollen breasts more than once in her attempt to get me to have sex with her. Jasper was mesmerized. He was begging me to do touch her. When he put his mouth on her nipple to try her milk like she suggested I told her to leave.

Instead, Hilda had straddled Jasper's lap. He was ready to fuck her right there with no concern for his life if my father came downstairs. He had told me I needed to taste her which disgusted me. She was possibly the mother of my son and she tried to get two sixteen-year-old boys to have sex with her while a nanny took care of Wills.

I had to stand, point at the door to the stairs and threaten if she didn't get her ass out of the room that I would call my father. That worked—Jasper didn't want anything to do with my father's temper and Hilda had all but run out of there.

Later that night, Jasper asked me if I'd fucked her before. I told him I hadn't. I wasn't admitting to that to him or anyone.

He didn't ask me about Wills until he turned two years old.

Wills looked exactly like me. It wasn't obvious or abnormal to anyone else because we were half-brothers. However, my father's unsaid accusations were obvious. He would glare at me and I knew he wondered.

Hilda soon became another ex-wife and my father's newest girlfriend was even younger—only a few years older than me. According to the prenup Hilda had signed without even reading it, Wills was to remain with my father. She could have fought him in court. She was his mother and the prenup was ridiculous. She never debated and left her son there. She rarely even sees him to this day on her designated weekends.

Wills was living my life and I hated it. I didn't want that for my son. Wills didn't have a Geraldine to come along to fill in the loneliness and isolation. He had a stepmother who acted as if he was a hindrance. She never wanted him around and swore she wasn't having kids. The idea of her stomach being anything but flat was unacceptable to her.

I grabbed Wills' photo album from my closet and took it with me to the living room to look over his photos. I'd taken him to the Central Park Zoo and a movie while I was in Manhattan. He'd talked nonstop about his new school and his new friend George. I listened as he shared every aspect of his life with me. I understood his babbling. When Geraldine would take care of me as a child, I talked to her like this. I had needed someone to listen about my life and to care.

When I dropped him of later that day, he'd held my neck tightly and told me he loved me. The hunger to be loved and wanted was so familiar to me. I'd been that child once. Taking him and running was so damn tempting. But I knew my father would have Wills within hours and I'd be thrown in jail. I had to fight my father the right way. I had to be smart. And if Wills wasn't my child, I had to find a way to save him anyway. A life with my father would ruin him. I didn't want him to be like me—hard, cold, unable to trust. He still had joy in his eyes, they held hope for more. That would eventually get beat out of him and I had to save him before that happened.

If he was mine, I would never be able to forgive myself for leaving him. Even though I had been a victim. I was just a fifteen-year-old boy that succumbed to a thirty-year-old woman sucking his dick and offering sex to him. It had been a mistake that possibly made me responsible for bringing a life into this world, only to hand him off to a life of hell. I didn't regret Wills' life. He was a great kid, but the circumstances he'd been born into could very likely be my fault.

When you're fifteen, you don't think about the circumstances that might result from your actions. I had been horny and in lust with Hilda. She was the adult and her actions should have concerned her, but she didn't cared. She only wanted what made her feel good. It was always about her and what she wanted.

Wills suffered because of that.

I had cursed myself thousands of times over the years for being so damn thoughtless. Berating myself wouldn't change anything. What had been done was done. I had to save him now.

My whiskey wasn't gone, but it was low. Shay had left a few glasses in the bottle. I poured one and walked out to the balcony. The night air was warm as I looked out into the darkness. Wills had never been to Savannah. I'd never been allowed to take him outside of Manhattan. He'd like it here. I'd made a list of things I wanted to take him to see. I'd told him about the city more than once. He would listen with his eyes wide with wonder.

The door behind me opened, and I turned to see Beulah walking out in nothing but the shirt I had been wearing earlier.

"Are you okay?" She yawned and her hair was messy from sleep.

When she was near me, I was okay. Touching her, being near her, it always helped. She made me forget for a moment. She reminded me of happiness. She showed me that life could be bright.

I set my drink down and held a hand out to her. She slipped her hand in mine and I pulled her toward me. She came willingly. Without saying anything I moved her to face the railing and then slipped my hands up her hips to find her naked underneath the shirt. Without direction, she widened her stance and put her hands on the iron railing in front of her and lifted her bottom up.

Rubbing my hand from her backside to the front, my fingers dove into her wetness. Her body responded to my touch with a jerk and she moaned. Playing with her for only a moment, I watched her wiggle and squirm. The sounds she made and how she felt as I commanded her with my hand had me so damn hard I couldn't take anymore. I pulled my erection from my boxers I guided it to her open warmth that waited for me.

Her loud cry as I entered her hard and swift was exciting. Taking her outside with her sounds of pleasure echoing in the night around us, I lost myself with each thrust. She was what fixed me. She was what would be my healing.

Chapter Ten

BEULAH

WAKING UP ALONE in Stone's bed after the past couple of days had caused me to panic. Finding him alone on the balcony with a glass of whiskey made him appear so vulnerable. Now that I knew his secrets I understood how deep his pain went. It wasn't just a childhood of mental and physical abuse. There was more, so much more.

As the night breeze warmed my skin, I let go of my inhibitions. I wanted to be whatever Stone needed. If giving myself to him out here in the open gave him relief, I would do it without hesitation. With each thrust he filled me, and slowly our actions had become a basic instinct. My body hummed with pleasure and the promise of release. I gripped the railing and my head dropped between my shoulders as I let the thrill of such a carnal exhibition wash over me. I didn't care if we are seen. I only cared about climbing for that apex. The moment the world would fall off balance and I'd go with it.

Stone's hands ran down my body and his fingers bit into the flesh of my thighs. Although it stung it caused me to buzz with desperation. I heard myself beg him. It was as if I were standing back watching us. He had torn his shirt from my body leaving me completely naked and bent over in front of him. My legs were spread wide and my face was a mirror of the passion as he drove into me relentlessly.

"I missed this." His voice was hoarse and strained. "You can fucking beg all you want, but I won't give you what you want until I'm ready."

I whimpered and bounced back against his pelvis. My bottom slapping him where we came together. "That's it," he encouraged me. "Keep giving me that pussy."

He leaned over and his hands slid down my chest until he was squeezing my breasts, feeling the heavy weight of them. He squeezed tightly and I moaned with pleasure. The sensitive tips pressed against his palms while his harsh breaths hit the back of my neck.

"I want to feel you come on my dick," he said close to my ear. "Then when you've got all you can handle I'll pull out and cover your ass with my come."

I shook as the image he painted propelled me closer to the edge. "Yes." I panted wildly.

"You want that?" he asked as his hands continued to pump and tease my breasts.

"Please." I was begging again.

"I'm so damn close. Come for me, baby." His deep voice was tense. As if holding back was painful.

His hands grabbed my hips and he slammed into me hard while I launched over the crest I'd been promised. Grabbing the rail to keep from falling I called out his name over and over. My knees buckled, but his hands kept my bottom up. Just as I began to slowly come down he pulled back roughly with a loud growl and the warmth of his release covered my backside.

"Fuuuuck!" was the only other word he spoke as he spasmed behind me. His hips jerking and his legs pressed against mine causing my already pleasured parts to start tingling again. I wanted to see him like this. Undone and free.

His arms wrapped around me right before I was lifted into his arms. He carried me back inside and closed the door behind us. I looked up at him. The angles of his face didn't seem as harsh as they had earlier. I had done that. My chest felt warm with the thought.

He carried me into his room and straight into his en suite. The massive shower had no door. I prepared for the cold water to hit me when he reached forward to turn the water on, but he held me back a moment. Before I thought it possible, he stepped under the warm water and let it cascade over both of us.

I was gently lowered until my feet touched the tile. Water ran over our bodies and I stood there looking up at him. Emotion set in at the reality that this was mine. I hadn't lost him. Moving on and finding a way to live without Stone wasn't going to be something I had to face. He was here.

"I'm going to bath you and try not to fuck you in the process," he said simply.

I perked up at that one word. But only nodded.

He reached for body wash and poured it into his hand before creating lather. He proceeded to massage the suds into my arms, stomach, breasts, and my back. I had to close my eyes to keep from getting worked up. Although I couldn't see him, it didn't help when his hands were moving between my legs.

I couldn't restrain the small cry that resulted from his touch. The sound I made caused him to pause. I widened my stance and he began again. I rocked my hips against his hand as it slid between my legs. He held his hand and fingers there, not moving. I took advantage of his fingers, rubbing my aroused sex until I had to grab onto his arms from the euphoria.

I was so close when he pulled his hand away to lift and press me against the shower wall. He entered me before letting me slide back down and I sighed with relief. This was what I wanted.

"More? I can't give you enough, can I?" His tone was excited.

"Never enough," I agreed readily.

He didn't move faster. Instead, he moved slowly inside me. Our eyes locked as he brought us closer and closer to the peak we both hungered for.

"I want to come inside you so goddamn bad, but I won't. We can't tempt fate again." He was strained, fighting his ache. The idea of locking my legs around him and holding him inside me was there in my thoughts. But I knew I wouldn't. We couldn't continue to do that as amazing as it felt.

He lowered his head until his forehead touched mine and I felt the slight tremble of his body. I let go, sobbing his name as I reached my orgasm. He held my tightly and I shook again and again unable to stop wave after wave that came over me.

Just when I thought I'd pass out, he pulled out of me and shouted as his warm semen shot against my thigh.

We stood there, both in a daze. The water was hitting our skin while our breathing slowly returning to normal. Neither of us moved. I didn't want to let go of him. I also didn't think I had the energy to walk. I was blissfully drained. The intensity from the past couple of hours had zapped me of all I had. It was beautiful. It was perfect.

When Stone finally moved it was to continue washing me. His hand was quick this time when he slid it between my legs. He didn't dwell too long on any sensitive area. I smiled with my eyes still closed.

The water cut off and he wrapped a thick towel around me. I held it tightly as I followed him out of the shower. A towel hung on his hips and his hair was still damp. Water was dripping from mine. None of that mattered. All I wanted was the bed and several hours of sleep. I was ready to relax.

Stone held back the covers and I climbed inside the bed. His body came in behind me and held me against him as I quickly fell into a deep restful sleep.

Chapter Eleven
STONE

SCANNING THE RESTAURANT, I found her easily enough. Hilda hadn't changed much over the past six years since Wills' birth. Men still turned their heads to watch as she passed. The excitement for life, however, was now void in her eyes. Coldness had taken the place of the once youthful gleam that had resided there. A reality that living with my father would do to anyone. My mother also had the same hardness in her gaze, although I'd never known what she was like before my father ruined her.

Walking toward Hilda, I feared this conversation would end the way the last few had. My lawyer was adamant that I attempt to get her to work with us one more time. I was done dealing with her, but I needed her cooperation to fight what was to come.

She lifted her gaze and a tight smile touched her red lips before she took a sip of her champagne. This meeting had taken me several calls to arrange. Hilda was currently living in Chicago as a congressman's mistress. The diamonds on her ears and the ones dangling from her wrist told me he was keeping her happy.

Taking the chair across from her, I sat down.

"Winston," she said in acknowledgment.

"Hello, Hilda."

"I would like to say that it's nice to see you, but we both know that's a lie." Her smile was gone replaced with a smirk.

"Thanks for agreeing to meet me. It's important."

She shrugged. "It's pointless, Winston. You know it is. Why you keep battling this, I don't know. It's a waste of your time and money. He'll never give Wills up."

I didn't expect him to. But if Wills was mine, I would take him.

"Life with my father is a living hell for anyone. You know that. How can you so easily accept the fact he has Wills? As a mother, don't you want to protect him?" I asked this knowing the answer already. Hilda was selfish. She only cared about her plans. Wills wasn't included in those plans.

"I didn't want to be a mother, Winston. You know that. I wasn't cut out to be a mother. I'm not the motherly type."

I grimaced. She sounded so much like my mother. The damage Wills had already suffered because of her and my father would be hard to repair. Every day he spent in that house, it only grew worse. I didn't want him to have my life. He deserved more.

"Obviously."

She looked at me with a bored expression and continued drinking her champagne. "When was the last time you saw Wills?" I asked.

She frowned. "I think in April, maybe?"

Wills had told me it was February since she'd last visited him. She'd patted his head and talked on her phone the entire visit. I wanted him to talk about how she treated him and how it made him feel. My hope was having him face it would keep him from withdrawing and letting the bitterness darken him. As it had me.

"You don't care what happens to him. You've made that clear. But I do. Even if he's my brother I don't want him to grow up the way I did. I've got to save him."

She lifted her left shoulder slightly. "You turned out just fine. Successful. Happy."

I laughed. My laugh held no amusement but disgust. She honestly thought I had turned out fine. Because I had been successful? The shallowness that consumed this woman was hard to be around. I didn't want to talk to her. If I could do this without her I would. But she was Wills' mother.

"Success doesn't equal happiness, Hilda."

She raised her eyebrows as if what I'd said was ridiculous. "Winston, you have never wanted for anything. Not once. I was cold in the winter, I went to bed hungry every night, and my clothes were either made by my mother or they were found in trash bins, thrown out by others. I lived in poverty. I watched my mother die from a cough that eventually consumed her in a cold, little one-bedroom shack. That is real fucking life. What Wills has is everything I didn't. I love my son and I know that he has more than I ever imagined having."

I'd never known anything about Hilda's youth or family. And although that was a sad story I still asked, "Did your mother try to keep you warm? Did she beat you or call you names to belittle you? Did she take care of you when you were sick? Did she love you?"

I stopped and waited for her to respond. Hilda tensed and I watched as she took a deep breath through her nose. I'd hit a nerve. She finally gave me a tight nod. That was it.

"Yes, she beat you? Or yes, she took care of you the best she could? She loved you?"

Hilda cut her eyes away from me. "She did the best she could."

"Did you feel loved?" I repeated.

There was no response for several seconds. When Hilda finally turned her gaze back to me she said, "Yes. But love didn't feed me or keep me warm. Love didn't give me a fortune."

She was right about one thing. I'd never been cold or hungry.

"A child needs love just as much as they need warmth and food. The lack of love damages you. I want Wills to feel loved. I don't want him hiding for fear his father will get angry with him and use his fists. That fear never goes away, even as an adult that can easily handle himself. It's there in your nightmares reminding you that you were weak once. You were alone."

Hilda sighed and took the napkin from her lap and placed it on the table in front of her before she stood up. "I can't keep doing this with you. We are not going to agree on what is best for Wills. If he's your son, I know he'll have just as much advantage in this world than if he is your father's son. Do whatever you think you must. But leave me out of it. I gave Wills up before he was born. That pre-nup made sure of it."

Hilda picked up her purse and tucked it under her arm.

"I swabbed the inside of his mouth while he slept during my last visit. I'll know If he is my son or my brother soon," I told her. "If he is, I will fight for him. If he isn't, I will still fight. If you won't, I will."

She gave a nod. "Like I said, do what you think you must. Goodbye, Winston."

I sat there as she walked away. I'd flown to Chicago hoping I could persuade her to stand with me in court. Having Wills' mother there testifying against my father would be huge. However,

I knew that was a long shot. Hilda hadn't been cooperative any of the other times I'd tried to get her with Wills. Even after she'd been on the receiving end of my father's fist. She knew how brutal he could be.

Standing, I laid money to cover the check on the table and left.

This was my last chance to get her on board before I moved forward either way. I would know tomorrow, if not sooner. They'd assured me the express test would take no longer than seventy-two hours.

If Wills was my son, I'd probably never forgive myself for not saving him sooner. The pain of that reality would haunt me. Forever.

Chapter Twelve
BEULAH

A SHORT NOTE. That was all I had from Stone. All it said was, I'll be home late.

Nothing more. No reason why. He hadn't even added an "I love you." Maybe it was girly of me to thinking that, but I hadn't heard from him all day. And I get home and find that note.

I hadn't eaten dinner with Geraldine thinking I would cook something for us tonight. We could have a nice meal together and talk about our day. I wanted to be there for him to discuss what his next steps were with Wills.

Nope. I was alone. With no information other than he would be home late.

Sitting in the kitchen, I ate a bowl of chicken noodle soup I had found in the pantry and heated up. There was nothing appetizing about canned noodle soup, but I wasn't going to cook just or me. The saltine crackers helped the taste somewhat. My plans to make spinach and chicken gnocchi for a nice dinner were now gone.

The apartment was quiet. I'd been here with it empty except for me more than I had been here with Stone. At least it seemed that way. I was being whiny. I knew my roaming thoughts were unreasonable, but I couldn't seem to stop myself.

Life with Stone was never going to be predictable or normal. I shouldn't expect it to be. Especially now. He had a lot on his shoulders. More than I could imagine. I had to be his support not another responsibility—he didn't need that.

Pausing mid-bite, the soup suddenly smelled funny. My mood was more than likely the cause. I stood up and walked to the sink to dump the soup, washed it down the sink disposal. A bath sounded nice. I would do that while I waited on Stone. Eating wasn't enjoyable.

After I washed my bowl and put it away, I headed to the room I had been sleeping in and decided I would use that bathroom. It felt weird going into Stone's bedroom and personal space without him here. This wasn't my home. I was referring to it as if it were, but this was Stone's home, not mine. I didn't have a home.

Stopping to look at myself in the mirror, I wondered if I should think about getting a place of my own. Stone had never mentioned that he wanted me to live with him permanently. We were . . . we were a couple. But that didn't mean he planned on us living under the same roof. Feeling displaced was normal for me, but it didn't make it feel less lonely. It made me miss my mother and our home.

Would she approve of Stone? I hadn't thought of that. I'd been so wrapped up in how he made me feel that I didn't stop and think about what my mother would have done in this situation. I had never seen her date or get serious with a man. Heidi and I had been her center. Her world. Had she ever been lonely? As a mother of two girls with no help, having a life outside of us had to be incredibly hard. She had no one to lean on, no support.

Once again, I was reminded of how tough my mother was. She was strong. She had raised me to believe in myself and to never depend on someone else. She'd taught me to change a tire, fix a lawn mower, climb a ladder to check the roof, and never think I needed a man for anything. And here I was feeling lonely without a man. I was vulnerable where I had been raised never to put myself in this situation.

The man who donated part of my DNA never came around. He never asked about me. Never helped her once. And I never heard her complain, mention him, or blame him for the difficulties I know she had to face. It was as if he never existed.

I walked into the bathroom and turned on the water for my bath. I would never be as tough as my mother. I could blame that on the unknown man who helped give me life. He was weak. Maybe that was where this emotional outcry was coming from.

With a sigh, I took off my clothing and stepped into the warm water. My head was all over the place. My emotions abnormally raw. It wasn't like me to worry and get worked up so easily. Stone has a job. He can't be expected to be here with me all the time. That was silly and I needed to get over myself.

Lying back, I closed my eyes and enjoyed the warmth of the water. My body was tired and my thoughts quickly began to ease and drift. Drowsily, I realized I was beginning to dream and forced my eyes open. I'd never gone to sleep in the bath before. Last nights events must be catching up to me.

My lack of sleep could also be contributed to my emotions. I sat up and started to wash my body deciding I needed to get some sleep before Stone got home. If he wanted a repeat of last night, I was on board. However, in order to keep up with him I needed sleep. At the thought of grabbing a nap, I yawned and my eyes watered. Jeez, I was tired.

I quickly finished and dried my body with a towel. I felt so out of sorts. Reasons for my off behavior ran through my head. I smiled when I realized it was probably time for my period. I paused and did the math in my head but it didn't seem right. Thinking harder I counted the days but once again it was wrong. It couldn't have been thirty-six days since my last period. I was a twenty-eight days on the mark girl. Never a day early or late.

My heart began to thud more rapidly in my chest. I wrapped the towel around me and searched for my phone. I needed to see my phone calendar because I had marked down the first day of my last period. I always marked the calendar so I knew when to expect my next one. Each step I took to my phone, my mind began assaulting me with what ifs I tried to slap away and push back.

When I grabbed my phone, my hand was trembling. I was shaking as I unlocked the screen and scrolled for the calendar app. There was a moment of pause before I clicked it. I wasn't sure I wanted to see. I wasn't sure I was ready if I wasn't wrong. Too much would be in the balance. I began to sweat as I lowered my thumb to press the small calendar app and it opened in front of me.

I closed my eyes and whispered a brief "please no" to God or whoever was out there listening.

With the panic causing my blood to pound through my veins so loudly I could hear it in my ears, I opened my eyes. The moment they focused and I studied the dates in front of me, I knew.

I don't know when I sat down. The floor had to be cold, but I didn't notice. My knees buckled and I went down like a tree falling. I was sitting on the floor staring at the phone in my hand. My mind was racing and my heart was beating so rapidly that my breathing became erratic.

All I could think about was a little boy who needed saving from a monster. Stone was facing the hardest battle of his life. The darkness from his past clawed away at his mind so much it haunted him. He was ready to save that little boy.

This was not what he needed. It was bad timing—the worst.

We had both known. When we chose to get lost in the pleasure, take a chance, we had been aware that this could happen. I hadn't thought about the consequences, and as the truth sank in, I wasn't thinking about them now.

I dropped my phone into my lap and touched my stomach with both hands. If there was a child inside, if we had created a life, I would love and cherish it. I'd never let my child believe I hadn't wanted it or that it hadn't been planned.

I wasn't sure I could stay here. My trust in Stone wasn't as strong as I thought it was.

At this moment, I couldn't say with certainty that I trusted him to want . . . this baby.

Chapter Thirteen
STONE

I DIDN'T WAKE Beulah when I finally got home. I hadn't planned on being so late, but my flight had been delayed for three hours.

When I walked in at midnight, she was curled up in the bed in the room I'd given her instead of mine. I didn't want to risk moving and waking her, so I had climbed into bed with her. In her sleep, she had curled up against me and mumbled something I didn't understand.

She would expect an explanation this morning. As well she should. I had planned on recapping my evening when I arrived home. However, the flight delay kept me from that conversation until this morning.

The coffee perked and the smell filled the kitchen as I watched the sun slowly rise through the windows. It was something I was accustomed to. Standing in a kitchen, drinking my coffee as the sun comes up. The difference was I had a woman I loved in bed.

I should be in bed with her still.

My eyes had barely closed all night. Instead, I was going through all the different scenarios that could transpire when the results from the DNA test came back. From the moment Wills came home from the hospital, he had felt like my sibling. But I'd always felt the weight on my shoulders that he could be my child. The reality I was forced to accept was that Hilda had decided my father would be Wills' father. Even after he beat her ass when she'd confronted him about sleeping with the college-aged daughter of one of his clients.

The designer clothing line that filled our stores should have been more important than a fucking vagina. Virginia was as empty-headed as a spoiled heiress could be, but my father hadn't been able to keep his hands off her. Now she was my stepmother. Hilda was thirty-seven and as far as my father was concerned she was over the hill.

I'd hoped she would at least seek revenge when he had divorced her. She hadn't. She'd taken his threats to heart and given up on being a mother to Wills. Disgusted with my train of thought, I grabbed a cup more aggressively than needed and poured my first cup of coffee.

I couldn't change Hilda. I couldn't rewind to before I had slept with her. That was done. And Wills was here.

"What time did you get home?" Beulah's voice was still raspy from sleep. I'd been so wrapped up in my thoughts I hadn't heard her in the kitchen behind me. That wasn't like me. I was normally very attune to everything around me. I turned to see her standing there in her faded and worn pink pajamas. Her mother had given them to her and she wore them for security. I realized she must have needed them last night and I knew it was my fault.

I sat my cup down and walked to her. "Midnight. I didn't realize it would be so late or I would have called."

She didn't relax. There was tension in her shoulders. As if she needed to protect herself. I slid a hand around her waist and pulled her to me before pressing a kiss to the top of her head. Still the stiffness remained.

"I went to see Hilda. My flight was delayed three hours. I expected to be home by nine. I was going to tell you all about when I came home, but that wasn't how it went."

She tilted her head back and gazed up at me. "Is she going to help?" Although her body remained tense she was truly concerned. Her eyes were so damn expressive she didn't need to speak for me to know what she was thinking.

"No," I replied. "She's not."

Beulah sighed and her frown deepened. "I'm sorry."

"Me too. I didn't expect her to but I had to try one more time."

"What are you going to do?"

I was waiting on the DNA results. I thought I knew what I'd do next but I also wasn't sure exactly how I would react if I was told Wills was my son. I couldn't leave him with my father another day. Knowing that taking him would be the worst move where my father was concerned, I feared I had to find another way to carry out my plan.

"I want to say I know this answer, but I don't. I will have to wait and see."

"When will you know?"

"Any day. Possibly today."

Beulah laid her head on my chest for a moment. Something was still bothering her. But she was holding it close. Not wanting to say anything, I would give her time to tell me what was on her mind on her own. If she didn't come out with it soon, I'd push until she told me.

"I don't understand mothers like Hilda."

She wouldn't. She had an excellent mother. A selfless one. It was rarer in my world than she realized. I wish every kid could have a mother like hers. A mother like I knew she would one day be.

"He deserves more than Hilda. She's better out of his life than in it." And I meant that.

"Every kid needs a mother," Beulah replied.

"I agree but not every mother deserves a kid." I'd seen that too many times.

Beulah pulled back and started to say something when my cell phone started ringing. She closed her mouth and her eyes widened. It was early. Too early for calls. I reached into the pocket of my flannel pajama pants and pulled it out. Glancing at the screen panic set in as Wills' name lit up the screen.

"Hey, bud." I stepped back from Beulah because the anxiety made me want to pace.

"Did I wake you up?" he asked with concern way beyond his years. Living with my father and no mother to care for you made you grow up fast. Already Wills was more reserved than the other kids his age. The sadness in his eyes mirrored what I'd once seen in mine when staring at my reflection. I hated it. I didn't want that for him.

"Not at all. You know I get up before the sun." I tried to sound cheerful. He didn't call me often. I checked on him more than he reached out to me. When I did get him on the phone, he rarely talked. It was more of a stinted conversation, if not completely one-sided. I always had to force him to chat by asking questions.

"Mom's coming today." He sounded unhappy about seeing

her. My grip on the phone tightened. Hilda hadn't mentioned that yesterday.

"You looking forward to seeing her?" I asked knowing he wasn't. He wished he was and I understood that feeling too. I wanted to enjoy my mother's visits, but I was afraid to want her. Afraid to care because she would leave and wouldn't return for a long time. It hurt and I didn't want to hurt. Wills was learning that young like I had.

"No." He sounded guilty for saying it. He needed to remember that Hilda's visit was fleeting, she was only passing through. He didn't need to get too attached her or hope for more? It seemed impossible to convey that to a six-year-old.

"She misses you," I said instead.

He grunted.

We were silent a moment while I tried to think of the right words.

"When will you be back?" he asked.

"I can be there when you need me," I told him.

He didn't say anything and I waited. He was trying to be tough.

"Maybe next week sometime, I mean if you get extra time and can." I knew that tone. I read between the lines easily.

"I'll see you in two days," I told him.

"Okay." And there was the first smile in his voice. For now, I'd have to be good with that. In two days, I'd know what I was going to do. I would know if Wills was legally my son or my brother.

Either way, I was saving him. I just didn't know how.

Chapter Fourteen
BEULAH

GERALDINE WAS DRESSED in an ice-blue ball gown made of satin and lace when I arrived the next morning. She kept telling me that the shrimp cocktail was unacceptable and that it was past time for the ice sculptures to arrive. I played along because this seemed to be a stronger spell than normal. She was anxious and frustrated and kept yelling at someone named Mona to get her satin slippers downstairs before the guests arrived.

When she slung open the fridge and wailed in a panic that the fruit salad wasn't even put together, I decided it was worse to let her believe this was real than to bring her back to the here and now. Closing the fridge door, I turned to Geraldine. "It's the year 2017. I'm Beulah and this is your home in Savannah. It's time for you to eat breakfast. I thought we'd have egg whites with goat cheese and a slice of tomato from your garden on a whole wheat English muffin." I spoke slowly and clearly hoping she understood and snapped out of it.

Geraldine stared at me in confusion for only a moment. She blinked several times before looking down at her dress. I almost sighed in relief that she was back when she made a disgusted grunt. "I wore this last year. Why did I forget that? I can't wear it again this year. This ball is too important. There are clients here, not just friends." She rolled her eyes and headed out of the kitchen and for the stairs. "If the ice sculpture arrives, tell them they're late and I want it by the fountain on the back patio." I walked over to watch her climb the stairs. At least she had calmed down. Maybe she'd come back around soon.

I thought about calling Stone, but I knew he had too much to deal with today. His mind was on other things. I could handle Geraldine. He needed less to worry about and this was all I could do to help him.

"Mona! Where are my riding pants? How can I hunt without them? Good Lord this is a mess!" Geraldine was yelling and she never yelled. Not even during a spell. Today was not a good day for her. I worried that she was getting worse.

"I'll look for them," I called back before she came running around the staircase upstairs looking for Mona.

While she went around upstairs looking for things from her past, I went back to the kitchen and worked on breakfast. Hopefully, she'd come back to me soon and I could feed her. The one thing about Geraldine being completely out of it since I had arrived was that it had gotten my mind off of me. Off of my problems.

Touching my stomach, I looked out the window and thought again about my doctor's appointment tomorrow. I'd originally made the appointment to get a prescription for birth control. Now? Now, I would be taking a pregnancy test. I would find out if I was already carrying Stone's child. Our child. A child that I would love and adore, but one that I knew he couldn't focus on right now.

The child inside me wouldn't ever face a life with the man who Stone hated the most. This child would have me always. He or she wouldn't have need for love because they would have it unconditionally.

Wills needed Stone and I wouldn't pull Stone in two directions. I wasn't sure of the right thing to do. Not telling him was wrong and he deserved to know.

Telling him right now when he needed his complete focus and attention on fighting his father was unfair too. I don't know how long I stood there silently lost in my thoughts. My thoughts swirled regarding I would do if I was pregnant. What I should do. What I needed to do.

"I don't even want to know why I was wearing that God-awful gown. It smelled of moth balls and I think I have a rash under my pits from the scratchy fabric," Geraldine said as she sauntered past me into the kitchen. I jumped at the sound of her voice. I hadn't heard her come back down the stairs.

She frowned at me. "Lord, girl. Are you okay?"

I smiled. "I didn't hear you come downstairs."

"I bet you smelled me though." She scrunched up her nose. "I must have been in the attic at some point this morning. That dress hasn't seen daylight in decades."

"It has held up well." I imagined the dress had been the height of fashion once.

She shrugged with her left shoulder only. "Perhaps, but now it is the height of ancient." She chuckled. "I'm a sight. You never know what you're going to walk into around here."

The smile that tugged on my lips this time was real. Not forced. Geraldine's spirit was always cheerful. Being near her made life seem easier. I was glad she was back from her spell. I needed her peaceful presence today.

"What's for breakfast?" She rubbed her hands together as she walked over to the coffee pot. I'd made coffee earlier hoping to coax her out of her memories.

I repeated the proposed menu.

"Oh, yum. I love that. It's my favorite. And my tomatoes are exceptional this year. I think it's the beer I used on them. I read about it on Pinterest. Do you ever go on Pinterest? It'll suck you in with its brilliant ideas."

I'd heard of Pinterest but couldn't say I'd browsed through the photos and ideas there. "No, but I know it's popular."

"It's bloody brilliant," she repeated with enthusiasm. "I bet you could find great ideas for cleaning, recipes, and the like. We should pull out my computer today and look at it together."

"Okay." I was grateful for something else to occupy my mind. I was desperate for anything.

"My friend, Beatrice, brought me some peppermint tea that I love. It can only be bought in England. I've tried a million different kinds here, but nothing compares. I even ordered some offline but it's not the same. This tea"—she held up a mesh bag of tea leaves—"is perfection. Something about the motherland I guess. The British know their tea. We just know our Starbucks." She sounded a bit disappointed. I knew she missed England. I thought it was because of her fond memories of her British friends that were gone from this world and of England that her mind always wandered back to that period.

"Do you want me to make you some tea to go with your breakfast?" I asked.

She shook her head. "Oh no. This is for tea time. It's British, darling. We need to have it at three."

She was teasing me, but then she was also serious. I poured her a cup of coffee instead. She had French coffee. As she swore by British tea, she also swore that the French were the coffee experts. I had to agree the coffee she had was amazing. There was nothing like it anywhere else.

"Where is my boy today? Haven't seen him in week." She changed the subject ever-so-subtly.

"He's dealing with work issues." I didn't know how much she knew about Wills. I didn't want to be the one to tell her the story. It was Stone's to tell.

Geraldine took the cup of coffee I handed her and her lips pursed slightly. "He's going to fight him, isn't he?"

I wasn't sure what to say here. I remained silent.

She let out a breath and tapped her fingertip on the counter. "I guess it's time. That child can't last the way Stone did. He's not as tough."

She walked toward the doors leading to the patio and said nothing more. I wondered what she knew. And if he had told her about Wills or she had just figured it out herself.

Again, I glanced down at my stomach and worried she may figure out my secret. What would I do if she did?

Chapter Fifteen
STONE

I MADE IT home before Beulah. Relieved after not seeing her car parked, I took my time getting my paperwork together and made my way toward the entrance of the building. I didn't want her to arrive home without me here again today. She seemed vulnerable last night and I wasn't sure why. It felt like she was going to bolt at any moment but couldn't make herself. With everything I had going on, I needed to make sure I found time for her too. I couldn't always expect her to be there for me and not reciprocate.

A car pulled up as I was unlocking the front door of my building and I turned to see it was a white Lexus. Whoever it was parked directly in front of me. I knew that Lexus didn't belong to anyone who lived here. Lifting my hand, I shaded my eyes from the sun to see who it was. Unfortunately, the tint on the windows hindered my view.

The driver's door swung open and Hilda stepped out of the

car. Hope, dread, and anxiety rushed through me at the sight of her. I wasn't dumb enough to think she had a complete change of heart after I had left her in Chicago yesterday. Her showing up here meant something though. I wanted to believe it was to help her son. I knew I was setting myself up for disappointment.

She flipped her sunglasses up on top of her head and made her way toward me. Each step she drew closer I wanted to ask why she was here. Instead, I waited. I'd asked, begged, and done all I could to help her. It was far-fetched to think she was here for my help now.

When she was only a few feet away from me she stopped.

"Wills called me crying. Your father has given him a real beating because he asked to come visit you." She paused and my hands clenched at my sides.

I'd hoped Wills would escape. My plan was to get him away before my father thought he was old enough to hit. That day had come too soon.

"I won't let him hurt Wills. He's a kind child. I'm ready to help. He needs free of that bastard."

Jumping on the first plane to New York to take Wills away was my first instinct. I knew I couldn't do that yet. I had to wait until I had all the facts straight. Messing up by letting my emotions control me would give my father the upper hand.

"Come inside." I turned and opened the door. Hilda followed me inside and we walked in silence up the stairs. I used every technique I'd learned over the years to calm myself. The rage boiling inside me was threatening to take over and right now I wanted to yell at the woman beside me. I was tempted to remind her that Wills wouldn't ever have had to suffer at the hand of my father if she'd been the mother he deserved. But her selfish behavior and choices had led us here.

Opening the door to my apartment, I stepped back and waved my hand for her to enter.

"Wow, Winston this is something else. Gorgeous. Stunning." Hilda was always impressed with material things.

"When did he call?" I was not interested in talking about my apartment with her.

She turned and I could see the subtle change in her demeanor. It had all kinds of warning signs attached to it. She was imagining something that would never be again. I didn't have the patience to deal with her stupidity.

"This morning around nine I was still asleep, but the phone kept ringing and I answered thinking it had to be important."

"It was," I stated.

She smiled. "Yes, it was. Anyway, he was crying. Upset. I calmed him down and we talked. He told me he wanted to come live with me." She batted her lashes and I watched as she worked up fake emotion and tears. I wanted to believe that she loved Wills, but I was sure I couldn't trust her.

"And if the results come back and he's not mine, he's my fathers. What then? Will you still fight for him?"

Her tears threatened to spill over. "Of course! He's hurting him, Winston!"

I'd warned her he'd hurt him from the beginning. When I wanted to know if he was mine. When I was a kid and had no power. But she didn't care then. "Why the sudden change of heart? This is something you've been warned about repeatedly."

She wiped at the tears yet to roll down her face. "I didn't believe you. Okay? I thought you were exaggerating or maybe you deserved what you got because you were a bad kid. I don't know," she trailed off. Sounding almost guilty for the words she was saying.

"I should have been the last person you thought would lie. I've never been dishonest with you. You can't say the same thing to me."

She opened her mouth to speak, took a step too closer and placed a hand on my chest. I reached for her hand to take it from my body and move her back.

At the same moment, the door to my apartment opened. I turned my head locked eyes with Beulah. I knew she would be here soon. Hilda showing up talking about Wills had distracted me and I'd forgotten momentarily.

"Who are you?" Hilda's tone was sharp. Possessive. As if she had some right to be in my home and ask who walked in my door.

I moved her hand away and walked to Beulah. Her eyes wide, confused, and nervous. This wasn't what she needed. Tonight, I had planned on talking to her about what had been bothering her.

"Who is she, Winston? We are dealing with family issues." Hilda's voice had gotten louder. I didn't respond to her. Instead, I kept my eyes on Beulah's. Reassuring her while the insane woman who was possibly the mother of my child ranted behind me.

"That's Hilda." I had dismissed Hilda for a second to stay focused on Beulah. She knew enough about Hilda to understand. At least I hoped she did.

"Is Wills okay?" she asked immediately. There was honest worry in her tone.

"He will be. But my father has hurt him. Scared him."

"Oh God." She covering her mouth. The pain shimmering in her eyes was real. It wasn't fabricated or worked up. She was genuinely worried about Wills.

"Why does she know about our son?" Hilda asked sharply. Demanding attention. Hating that she was ignored.

I slipped my arm around Beulah's waste. "Beulah meet Wills' mother, Hilda. Hilda this is my girlfriend, Beulah. She lives here. With me."

She hadn't been expecting a girlfriend. That much was obvious. There was a certain annoyed gleam in her eyes that I read all too well. Women like Hilda wanted to be the most important. The most beautiful. Beulah was sixteen years younger and by far more beautiful inside and out. Hilda would hate that.

"It's nice to meet you," Beulah said. Her voice was sweet and perfect.

Hilda glared at her but only for a moment. She snapped out of her snit quickly and forced a smile. A smile that was all too vibrant. "Likewise. I am sure we'll be fast friends."

I doubted that.

Chapter Sixteen
BEULAH

"**I DIDN'T KNOW** she was coming here," were the first words out of Stone's mouth when we stepped into his bedroom.

"I'd figured that out," I told him. It was obvious he'd been caught off guard, butut there was hope in his eyes. Hilda showing up here was a good thing for Wills. They had to work together to help him.

Stone ran a hand through his hair messing up his thick locks. "I need her help. Wills needs her help. Honestly, I don't want her here with us . . . staying in my place. Our place. She's toxic." He was worried about me and I knew that. I could tell within seconds of entering the apartment that he was on guard where Hilda was concerned. He was ready to swoop in and save me. I wasn't that helpless. I knew I could deal with Hilda. Just because I was nice didn't make me weak.

"We will be fine with her here. This is a good thing. A very good thing. Don't worry about anything else. You have enough to be concerned with."

He walked over to me and put both his hands on my waist. "I'm glad she's here. I'm not happy with what finally pushed her here. My stomach is in twisted in knots over it. But I have a chance now. I also have this." He reached into his back pocket and pulled out an envelope. Frowning, I looked at the envelope and tried to puzzle out what was inside.

"The results. I was waiting until we were alone to look at them. No matter what they say, what these results tell me, I will need time to adjust. Hilda showing up surprised me and I put look at this on hold."

We would both know now. The next steps he took would be decided by the results in that envelope. I was confused what my steps with be and wouldn't know until after my doctor's appointment tomorrow.

"Open it when you're ready." I didn't want to push him. I imagine in his heart and mind there was a lot riding on what the piece of paper inside that envelope said. Stone already loved Wills. He'd lived not knowing if he was his father, but that hadn't changed his love for him.

Wills and Stone had the same eye color, but the color wasn't rare. That didn't make Wills his. And the boy's dark hair and smile looked more like Hilda to me now that I had seen her. Sure, looking at the photos the boy could be his. But he could be his brother just as easily.

Stone stood there looking at the photo in his hands. His frown drawn tightly. So many things running through his head. I would make this easier on him if I could. But there was nothing I knew I could do. Nothing at all but stand here and be his support. He wasn't alone anymore.

At least not now.

His slowly opened the envelope and pulled out the neatly folded paper from inside. I looked up to find Stone was watching me. He took a deep breath as if to steady himself. I gave him an encouraging nod and he held the paper in his hand. The slight tremble didn't go unnoticed by me. It was another small glimpse at his vulnerability.

I wasn't sure if I was breathing as I stood there waiting for him to say something. The unknown had hung in the air for so long now that he knew it would change so much for him internally.

His hand didn't give way to the answer he was reading. His body didn't react differently. I searched for any clue as to what he knew. What to be prepared for. Wills' chance at a life free of that man would all weigh on this.

It seemed like an eternity as the room stayed silent. I didn't push. It wasn't my place. This would all be when Stone was ready to share. Finally, he lifted his head and his eyes said everything. They reflected his raw pain, the joy he felt, and the desperation. So many things all stemming from the same truth.

"He's mine . . ." There was a pause. A brief moment where he looked he was unable to speak. As if he wasn't sure he understood himself. I wondered what could have him so shocked. He knew that Wills was very likely his. There was something that was causing the look of disbelief on his face.

"He's not my father's son . . ." He repeated what I already knew. Confused, I could do nothing else but wait. He was still grasping mentally at something. A fact he wasn't prepared for. "Neither am I."

Those last three words caused me to pause and repeat them

in my head. Neither am I? I was confused. Neither is he what? His father's son? What he had said dawned slowly and I felt my jaw drop as everything sank in.

"Wills has none of my father's DNA. Not a trace. If he's my son, then he'd have some of my father's DNA too. He's unequivocally mine. He even has my blood type. His eyes aren't the only thing I gave him."

His voice was deep, hoarse with emotion. I took a step toward him and he shook his head as if he couldn't believe it. "He's not my father. The man I've grown up fearing, trying to please, and ended up hating was not the man who gave me life. He abused me. He damaged me. He taught me at a young age not to trust anyone. He kept me from finding any form of real relationship or even love until you."

I opened my mouth to say something, but he tossed the paper on the bed and let out a harsh laugh. One that had no humor. One so full of anger and disgust that I took a step back.

"She knew. My mother . . . she knew. She knew I wasn't his and she let me grow up under that man's fist. When she could have taken me. All she had to do was prove I wasn't his. That was it. But the money . . . that goddamn money. It was all that mattered. All that fucking mattered."

My heart was breaking as he spoke. The little boy he'd been was so desperate to be loved. He so desperately wanted to please that man. The one who hated him knowing he wasn't his son. Believing his own mother allowed it when she knew he could be free of the man seemed heartless. Even more so than Portia. At least she'd left her daughter with someone who would raise her with love and adore her. She was left with a mother that made sure she was always taken care of and secure.

"It's possible she didn't know?" I wanted to believe his mother didn't.

He didn't look at me. "She knew," he replied his voice void of emotion now. Where the pain had been it was now hollow.

Words didn't come. I wanted to say something to comfort him but nothing came to me. Instead I walked to him and wrapped my arms around his waist. The stiff body under my touch didn't relax. I could almost feel his emotions pulsing through him. Even now, as a man, he is forced to face the monsters of his youth.

The secret I might hold inside me would stay there for now. That's all I could do. Stone needed me to be strong and stay by his side. And that's what I would do.

Chapter Seventeen
STONE

HILDA DIDN'T COME out of her room until ten minutes after nine the next morning. I'd been pacing the living room floor trying to remain calm as different scenarios played out in my head. There was a good chance that the man I had thought was my father knew already knew he wasn't. He may also know Wills wasn't his son as well. I had to be prepared for that. I also needed to talk to Hilda to find out what she knew.

There was too much riding on all this and she chose to sleep in. She didn't seem worried at all about Wills.

When she finally came out of the room she was completely dressed, hair and makeup done. The scent of her perfume that had once made me a horny wreck now caused me to physically cringe. Regret was the only thing attached to that scent.

"Good morning," she said beaming brightly as if her little boy hadn't been left scared and alone. As if the child we had created didn't need to be rescued. She was taking her bloody sweet time getting dressed and now she was all smiles. My hands fisted beside me and I fantasized about putting them through a wall. My anxiety grew until anger began to take over.

"He's mine," I told her and waited to watch her reaction. I needed to know if she knew more than she had always let on.

She paused a moment. Her eyes shuttered and she smiled. "Good. That makes this easier, doesn't it?" Her response wasn't one of relief. It was more rehearsed than anything.

"Did you know?" I demanded. "I don't have time for fucking games. Did you know he was mine?" My voice was getting louder.

Her eyes flew open wide in response to my fury that was impossible to mask.

"How would I know, Winston?" Her hands went to her waist defensively. "I'd been fucking you and your father at the same time. I was stupid and careless. But he was old and I needed your youth and beauty. Your dick was always on go and ready to please me. He couldn't keep up with my needs. You did. I was wrapped up in his power and money, but I was addicted to fucking you. So no, I was never sure who Wills belonged to!" Her cheeks were pink and flushed. I could see the way she was moving toward me and the way her chest was rising and falling too quickly. It was obvious what she wanted. What she was thinking about. She definitely wasn't focused on Wills right now.

"But you didn't care either did you?" I shot back at her and moved away putting distance between us. I didn't want her close to me. Her choices, her selfishness . . . it disgusted me. However, her mental trip down memory lane had caused her to think about things she wanted and missed. Things I never wanted to experience again.

"I was confused, Winston. Scared. Your father is a powerful

man. I was doing what I had to in order to protect us both."

Again, no mention of Wills. As if his well-being was of no consequence to her.

"It seems you're not the only woman to marry the man and not be sure who had fathered the child she carried. My mother did the same thing. Who fathered me, however, is unknown. I'll have to ask her. What I do know is she left me with that man exactly like you left Wills. Not entirely sure if he was your child's father or not. But the money he gave you was more important than the welfare of your child." The pain my mother had caused was coming through and I was putting that on Hilda. And she deserved it. She'd done the same thing. They were alike—vain and self-absorbed.

"What are you talking about?" Her perfectly plucked brow barely wrinkled with the Botox I knew had to be under her skin.

"My mother was like you. She was fucking someone else while she was with my father. The DNA results came back and they didn't just confirm that Wills was mine," I paused and glared at her. I wanted to make sure she understood all of this. Every damn word. "Wills isn't his grandson either. There is NO blood relation to the man I always assumed was my father to Wills. Yet Wills is my son. So that tells you what?"

Her eyes rounded and her jaw dropped. She blinked several times. I let that information sink in. She covered her mouth with her left hand. I turned and walked away. Her candid shock only infuriated me more. This was all something I had forced. She'd never have pushed for me to check Wills paternity. I did that without provocation. I was the one who wanted to know. She didn't want Wills. Her showing up here had nothing to do with Wills, I knew that now. I saw past her shallow excuse.

"Why are you here, Hilda? What is it you want?"

She studied me for a moment. Truths and lies flashed in her eyes as she decided what it was she wanted to tell me.

"Tell me the fucking truth, damn you!" I roared in frustration.

She didn't back away. She didn't appear scared nor did she play the victim. Instead, she took a step toward me. "I came for you. I want you. You want Wills and I can help you get him. But I want you," she said the words as she ran a hand over her left breast. "We were good together, Winston. You know we were."

I stood there. Not much surprised me anymore. But this, at the moment she chose to pull this stunt, it was like slapping me in the face. More proof she cared nothing for our son. I'd created a child with a heartless woman. He had a mother much like my own and I'd done this. It was my fault.

"I will fight for my son with or without your help, Hilda. I have the power I need now. This idea you have that we can go back to what we had when I was a kid is stupid. Pathetic. It's also a waste of my time. I don't need you here. If you cared about Wills then I would respect your presence. But this . . . offer you've made? I don't want it. I don't think I can even stomach repeating it."

She threw her shoulders back as if she were born into money rather than married into it. "Because of that girl?" her words sounded bitter.

"That girl is the woman I have waited my life to love. She saved me."

Hilda rolled her eyes and sighed. "I thought you were smarter than that. Jesus, Winston. That's what is pathetic. No vagina is that good. You've had a lot of them. Don't tell me hers is magic."

This wasn't a conversation I was going to have with anyone, especially not Hilda.

"If you want to help with Wills, stay. But you better remember your reason for staying here and your place. If you want nothing more than to try and fuck me, leave now. You're wasting my time."

A large part of me wanted her to walk out the door. I feared her presence could hurt things with Beulah. I didn't trust Hilda, but she was Wills' mother. Even if she was a careless bitch, she was his mother. He needed to see her fight for him.

"He's my son. I'm staying."

Chapter Eighteen
BEULAH

GERALDINE HAD ASKED to go visit Heidi when I arrived this morning. She'd already made the cake batter and started making cream cheese icing when I walked in the door. The thought of seeing my sister made things seem brighter.

Leaving Stone's this morning I had felt as if we were drifting apart. I didn't have a reason to feel that way. And I was aware my insecurities were heightened after learning he was a father. It also didn't help that Hilda was staying in his house. Not to mention it was possible I was carrying our child. My emotions were all over the place.

Geraldine's idea was better. Focusing on Heidi was safe.

Lucky for me, Geraldine also had me making cookies because they were her grandmother's recipe and she knew Heidi and May would love them. That gave me even more to occupy my thoughts. It was almost lunch when we finished baking and Geraldine had put her final touches on everything.

I'd thought Stone might stop by, or I had hoped he would. Being apart was difficult right now. Things seemed so rocky and I had suddenly become needy. I didn't like that feeling at all.

"I have this beautiful pink dress with ruffles. You can twirl and the ruffles dance all around you. It's perfection. Do you think Heidi would like that? It's hanging in my closet. Every time I see it I wish someone could enjoy it the way I once did. We both know I'll end up prancing down here in it eventually when I'm in a crazy spell. Might as well give it to someone who can use it."

I didn't think Heidi could use a dress like that. Would she enjoy it though? Absolutely. She'd think she was a princess and I doubted she'd ever take it off. Which meant it would get dingy and stained. There is no telling how much Geraldine paid for the dress. Giving it to Heidi to play in made me nervous.

"I know she would love the dress, but I'm afraid she won't appreciate it. She'd want to play outside in it. There would be dirt stains and icing smears," I explained with a smile. The offer was incredibly generous. I didn't think Geraldine understood Heidi that well. Even after our visits.

Geraldine laughed and waved a hand. "Who cares about that! I want her to have fun in it. That dress was meant for fun. Excitement. Adventure. Not dust in an old woman's closet," she said then clapped her hands together. "I'm going to get it now. We're taking it with us. She can even wear it while she eats these cupcakes and cookies. It'll be the most excitement that dress has seen in decades."

I opened my mouth to argue, but Geraldine was gone. She was fast for her age, especially when she wanted to be. I watched as she ran up the stairs—or rather, walked swiftly. Going to visit Heidi always put her in a good mood. I was thankful for that because it did the same for me. I needed to see Heidi today. Her smile would ease the constant ache in my chest. The one that was foreboding, warning me the inevitable was coming.

This afternoon I would see my doctor. Geraldine already knew I was leaving early for an appointment. The closer it got to my time to leave for my appointment, the more nervous I became. I'd be there alone. Stone thought it was for a routine visit and to get me on birth control. I couldn't tell him I was having a pregnancy test. He had too much to deal with.

As hard as I tried, I couldn't stop thinking about him and Hilda alone. Together. I wondered what they were doing and what they were talking about. Was he still attracted to her? Did he remember what it was like to have sex with her and did he want to again? I sounded ridiculous but my curiosity was eating away at me.

"What shoe size does Heidi wear?" Geraldine asked as she came back down the staircase holding a pair of pink satin slippers. If they had been heels I would have been against it but the slippers were like ballet flats and Heidi would be fine in those. Her balance wasn't the best. Heels had always been hard for her. She'd twisted her ankle trying mine on before my graduation.

"Seven," I told her knowing the shoes she was carrying would fit perfectly.

"These are seven and a half," she beamed. "I wear an eight now. My foot has grown with age. But these feel like you're walking on a cloud. She'll love them."

"She won't know how to handle so much excitement. A surprise visit is one thing. We are also taking the treats, the dress and shoes. She's going to think it's Christmas."

Geraldine was smiling from ear to ear. She liked doing things for people. It was one of the many reasons she was easy to love.

She had a huge heart. Heidi had taken to her immediately. She'd be happy to see her again today.

"Has Stone visited Heidi with you?"

Her question made me pause. I didn't want to answer that. As imperfect as Jasper was, he'd visited Heidi with me. He knew she was important to me and he had wanted to be a part of my life. Stone had never asked or shown interest.

Again, my emotions were raw. I was being sensitive. Shaking that off, I smiled and mentally reassured myself that everything was fine. Stone was withdrawn, quiet, kept to himself. Jasper was different. He liked crowds.

Stone liked crowds too. Or at least it seemed like he did when he was at Jasper's parties. They had been his people though—the ones he'd grown up and gone to school with.

No. I would not do this to myself. I was digging up drama where there wasn't any. "Stone is busy. He rarely has time to sleep. I can't expect him to find time to visit my sister," I said knowing I didn't have to defend him to Geraldine. She understood him better than anyone.

"Humph." She frowning as we walked to the door. "He's got time to have relations in my pantry while he thinks I'm napping. I guess if he can do that he can visit your family with you."

I opened my mouth and closed it three times, unable to think of the right thing to say here.

"Stop flapping your jaw or a fly is gonna get in there. Now, come on. Let's go see your sister. I won't talk about Stone anymore today. But I will tell you this"—she stopped and looked at me—"you have got to make a stand. Let him know what you expect and deserve. Don't let him run all over you or take advantage of your good nature. He's a man, Beulah, and they are all a little self-centered until we shake them up a bit."

All I could do was nod. I didn't think Stone was self-centered at all, but I wasn't about to argue with her. She would keep going, and we would run out of time. I had three hours to visit with my sister and drive Geraldine back home to get her settled before my appointment.

"Men don't know how good they've got it when they find themselves a good one. We are worth our weight in gold." Geraldine marched toward the garage that housed her Mercedes.

I didn't comment.

"Do you think I should wear this pink dress to the Miller's wedding?"

I had no idea who the Millers were. I started to ask when she added "I can't believe Claudia is getting married so young. We have years left of our youth. What is she thinking?"

I slowed my pace and wondered if I should turn back to the house. I couldn't take Geraldine to see Heidi like this.

"I haven't rolled my hair yet!" Geraldine gasped before she turned and ran back to the house. "I can't go like this. Why didn't you tell me?"

I watched her walk inside the house. The cookies and cupcakes I was holding smelled good. I reached for a frosted sugar cookie and took a bite. I chewed slowly and waited. When Geraldine didn't come back, I knew she wouldn't be snapping out of this one anytime soon.

Visiting Heidi would have to wait.

Chapter Nineteen
STONE

GERALDINE WASN'T ANSWERING her phone. Beulah wasn't answering hers. It was after seven and the doctor's office closed two hours ago. Hilda was drinking my good wine and listening to a loud ass reality TV show in the living room.

And all I fucking wanted was to be alone with Beulah. Today had been hell.

Although my lawyers felt positive now that we had proof the DNA said Wills was mine and I had his mother ready to stand by my side to fight for him, they were still worried about the power behind my father's name . . . or the man I thought was my father.

Wills had called me today, and when Hilda asked to speak to him his entire tone changed. He was nervous. Tense. He didn't want to talk to her. She wasn't a source of comfort for him and I understood his feelings all too well. But Wills didn't have a Geraldine in his life.

I glanced at the clock again and decided I'd look for Beulah.

I couldn't stay here wondering where she could be. My pacing in front of the door wasn't helping anyone. Hilda's drunken laughter was also grating on my nerves. She had an affair back in Chicago she would need to get back to eventually. I didn't expect her to stay here long. As much as I needed her in court, I didn't need her in my home.

The door knob turned and I froze. My first instinct was to grab it and swing it open, but I waited for Beulah to open it up and walk inside.

She was barely in the door when I blurted out "Where have you been?" It was harsh, and demanding. I cringed at the tone of my voice. My worry and panic had built up and I couldn't help my reaction.

Startled, she jumped and stood there looking at me with eyes wide with fear. I hadn't meant to scare her. However, my damn voice had been too much.

"T-today was m-my doctor's appointment," she stammered.

"I know that. I've been counting down until this day. But the doctor's office closed at five. It's after seven."

Beulah still looked confused by the tone I was using. I was trying to soften it, but it wasn't working. I was letting my anxiety control me.

"Geraldine had a spell this evening. I couldn't leave her like that. I had to take her with me. She came back around while we were there. Instead of going back to her house and making her dinner she wanted to go out to eat. So, we did."

"Why didn't you call me to help? Or at least answer your phone? I've been worried."

"I should have. I'm sorry. You didn't call me earlier today and I thought you were busy. I had to turn my phone off at the doctor's office and forgot to turn it back on afterward. I'm so sorry. I didn't think you'd be home or I would have called to explain." Her tone was sincere but she was different. She seemed almost defensive. As if she wanted to yell at me, but was holding back.

"Were you expecting me to call earlier today?" I was trying to decide what it was that she was upset about, but wouldn't tell me. She'd hide it. Or attempt to.

"Only if you wanted to. I know you're busy." Her words were nice. Agreeable. But her tone, the look in her eyes said something entirely different.

"I should have called earlier. I'm sorry," I said thinking that must be it.

"It's okay. I'll keep my phone on from now on." Her head turned toward the living room where the noise from the television was coming from. We never had the television on in there. It was odd. Out of place. Not the normal evenings we had here. Hilda's presence was making both of us tense.

"Come with me." I held my hand out to her. She paused for a second, studying my hand. Finally, she placed hers in mine. I closed my fingers tightly and gently pulled her down the hallway toward my room.

I needed to get away from the reminder of Hilda. All that damn sound.

Closing the door firmly behind us, I turned to her and grabbed her waist to pull her against me. "Did you get the shot?" I asked wanting to be inside her without concern.

She didn't respond at first. I had a moment of disappointment. I'd been waiting for this day. I hadn't held back before, I knew, and we still had to be careful. Especially now. I had to fight for Wills. If something were to happen, she would need more support and attention than I had to give right now.

"It's safe," she said simply.

Pulling her to me I buried my head in her hair and inhaled. I soaked in her warmth and scent. As always, she calmed me and gave me the reassurance I needed.

The noise from the television was blocked out.

We were alone.

I took that moment to enjoy our solitude. Us.

Only for a moment.

I couldn't help the thrill I felt knowing I could shoot my release in her. The urge to take her was louder and more commanding than my other feelings at the moment.

I reached under the short skirt of her sundress, found her panties and pulled them down. She shimmied her hips, helping me until they fell down her legs and she stepped out of them.

Grabbing her waist, I picked her up and carried her to my bed and I tossed her onto it. Her legs fell open and her eyes followed my every move. I didn't have time for foreplay. Not this time. I had to get inside her—it reassured me that she was here and we were okay.

My pants were gone with ease and I climbed over her and eased into her as she lifted her knees and hips for easier access. Gliding through her slick warmth tore a groan of pleasure from me. I'd found myself thinking about this very moment several times today. Now we were here, and I didn't want to leave.

I grabbed her left leg and brought it over my shoulder making my penetration deeper. Everything felt more intense. Beulah's head pressed back into the soft bedding and she let out a cry. Then she said my name. Several times. I began to pump into her faster. I was excited by the idea of reaching my climax inside her making my movements become more frenzied.

I was like a fucking addict. Needing this fix.

"Stone!" She moaned and clawed at my back.

I pressed her tightly against me as the sound of our bodies joining faster and harder became louder. Her breathing had become a pant and mine was heavy and fast. Her arms were wrapped tightly around my neck as she met each of my thrusts, pressing deeper.

"Oh, oh, oh." Her climax was close. Her body began to shake and her nails dug into my flesh. The sweat on her thighs as her skin rubbed against mine made it fast and smooth. "I'm coming," she wailed and buried her head in my chest as I gave three more hard thrusts and yelled out my release.

She cried out, chanting my name as the heat from my seed filled her.

"Fuck, baby, that's it. Take it," I said pulling back on her hair so I could look in her eyes as I filled her. "Feel that?" I asked pressing deeper inside her.

"Yes." Her eyes were heavy and she was trembling. "It's hot."

I let out one last growl as I finished emptying into her. This was what I'd needed all fucking day. I felt better now. I felt fucking perfect.

Pulling her back into my arms I held her and we laid there until her breathing slowed. When I knew she was asleep, I closed my eyes and followed her.

Chapter Twenty

BEULAH

STONE WAS STILL asleep when I woke up the next morning. I stayed wrapped in his arms, staring out the window where the sun was about to rise. It was early and I'd slept all night. We hadn't moved since this was the exact position I'd fallen asleep. Sex had been amazing. I was more sensitive. I wondered if that was because of the pregnancy.

It was early still, but the urine test at the doctor's office confirmed I was pregnant. I didn't need to give blood to confirm. My period wouldn't come this month. I didn't know how I'd hide that. Stone wasn't the type to not want sex simply because I was bleeding.

Even now, with all these unknowns, with decisions I had to make, I wanted to turn over and open my legs for him to come inside me again. What was wrong with me? I was thinking about sex and I had a life to be worried about now.

My hand went to my still flat stomach.

Geraldine had come back to herself while we were in the waiting room so she stayed in the waiting room. As far as she was concerned, I was there for birth control. I didn't tell her anything else. However, having someone out there waiting on me had given me some peace. I hadn't been alone.

The joy when the doctor entered the room and congratulated me had been overwhelming. It had lasted only a few moments before reality sank in. Telling Stone was one of was going to be hard. I'd have to tell him eventually. How long could I wait? How long would the battle he was about to face going to last? I feared it was longer than nine months and waiting it out wasn't going to be an option.

His hand covered mine and I jerked in response. When he threaded his fingers through mine and pressed a kiss to the side of my head I relaxed. He was waking up. He hadn't been reading my thoughts. His hand over my stomach was only a reflex.

"Good morning." His voice was deep and husky from sleep. "Did you sleep as good as I did?"

"I don't think I moved." It was the first full night I'd slept in a few days at least.

He kissed my ear. "Me neither. But you're going to need a shower this morning. We went to bed messy." The smile in his voice as he said it made me laugh against the pillow.

"You think that's funny?" he asked as he lifted my leg and moved behind me.

I didn't have time to give him a response before he was inside me. Again. And it felt wonderful.

He took my leg and laid it over his hip as he rocked slowly in and out of me. I hadn't done it like this before. All I knew was that the angle was rubbing against something amazing inside me. It was that or I was so sensitive down there these days that anything touching me had my eyes rolling back in my head.

I moved my leg as high as I could, opening myself to him. Unable to stop myself I reached down and touched my clit. It was larger than normal and the sheer pleasure from just touching it caused my entire body to shudder.

"Fuck, keep doing that. Whatever it is your tight little pussy is squeezing my dick like a vice," he groaned in my ear.

I began to play with it as the moisture from our lovemaking leaked out making it slick and easy. Each brush of my fingers made me clinch Stone tightly and he in return made noises to let me know he approved.

"Are you touching yourself?" he asked in my ear.

"Yes," I admitted, unable to care. At this point, I'd get myself off while he watched if it meant I would get the orgasm building inside me.

"Jesus," he whispered and his hand covered mine. He didn't hinder me but he brushed his hand over mine as I continued my attention to the now pulsing spot under my fingers. "Keep playing," he panted.

He didn't have to worry. I never planned on stopping. I was too close. "Tell me when you're about to come," he said.

My body was beginning to draw tight. The explosion was coming. I wasn't sure I could warn him. My voice was gone.

I managed an—"I'm about to"—and his hand brushed mine out of the way. I cried out in frustration, but his hand had replaced mine and he pinched the tight needy ache sending me barreling into bliss.

His hips slammed into my backside as he held his hand on my clit. "Holy fuck!" he yelled out and the warmth of his release spread through me. Feeling him inside me sent my body into another climax. My cries met his, and we were lost in a state of beauty there together. Nothing mattered.

My orgasms had never been this intense. I didn't know there was another level to them. I wondered if it was from the pregnancy. I'd have to look it up later. But if this was a perk of pregnancy then I was going to become a nympho and I hoped Stone could keep up. Even now with my body exhausted from this mornings activity, I knew I'd be all in again if he tried. Thinking about him sliding in and out of me made me start to spark to life again and I had to squeeze my eyes shut tightly to stop myself.

"I'd bath you but if we get in the shower together you're not going to make it Geraldine's on time," he said with a chuckle.

I turned in his arms and smiled up at him. Right now, my worries weren't there with us. The time we were spending now was us in love. Happy. I had all day to think about everything else and how my pregnancy would affect us. Right now, I just wanted to enjoy Stone.

"I really like birth control," he said then pressed a kiss to my lips.

The reminder, however, was enough to shake off my sleepy state of euphoria. I didn't have a response for that because it would be lying and soon I was going to have to tell him the truth. I had to wait for a good time to tell him. He was dealing with too much at the moment and I wasn't comfortable telling him yet.

"I like that position," I said changing the subject back to the sex.

He hadn't pulled out of me yet. His erection wasn't completely gone and he made it twitch inside me. Startled, I laughed and he grinned wickedly at me. "You better get your ass out of this bed or Geraldine will be cooking her own breakfast.

The idea of shower sex sounded good to me, but he was right. I had to get ready for work.

"Will you be home when I get here tonight?" I already missed him. And I was feeling clingy again.

"You'll see me before then." He kissed my lips. "Now put some distance between your hot little pussy and my cock. Please. It has a mind of its own."

Giggling, I scrambled out of bed and ran to the shower.

For a moment life was beautiful. Simple. No secrets. Only for a moment.

Chapter Twenty-One
STONE

I SLIPPED MY phone in my pocket after speaking with my father. He still knew nothing and was currently in London dealing with the department store there. That specific store was newer and required more of his time. Making sure he was gone and putting a date on his return was my first step.

Marianna had let me in and directed me toward where I could find Wills. Marianna was the newest housekeeper/nanny. She was in her sixties and slightly overweight. Obviously, my stepmother had chosen her. I had to admit she was smarter than the stepmothers. If she had left it up to him, Marianna would have a stripper name and be younger than her with larger breasts and looser morals.

A bonus was that I liked Marianna and so did Wills. She wasn't motherly, but she was kind. He needed that in this place. Especially now that he was considered old enough to get hit by the man who thought he had the right.

I knocked on the door to the game room once and slowly opened it. Wills was sitting crossed legged on the sofa with a remote control in his hand. A video game played out on the large screen in front of him—it was motorcycle racing. The music was loud on the game and he hadn't heard me knock or come in.

"No!" he yelled at the game. "Not NOW!"

I watched as the motorcycle's tire blew out and it spiraled out of control.

"Son of a bitch!" He threw the remote down.

I cleared my throat and he swung his head around. When he saw it was me, his first expression was surprise that quickly morphed into a smile taking over his face. Everything about seeing him today was more. I didn't think I could love him more than I already did. But standing there, looking at him and knowing he was mine, I realized I'd been holding a piece of myself back. Protecting it in case I found out he wasn't my son. Now my chest felt like it was going to explode as I walked toward him.

"Stone!" He jumped up and ran toward me. His arms were in the air and the mouth that had spoken in a tone too old for his age was now gone. The six-year-old boy was throwing himself into my arms, completely confident I would catch him.

"Hey buddy." I picked him up and hugged him tightly. Emotion clogging my throat. I closed my eyes a moment to mentally get a grip. I wanted to take him and run. Rescue him from this place. Hide him from the ugliness he'd already witnessed.

Knowing I couldn't take him now made it so damn hard to stand here and not fucking weep. He was just a little boy. A kid. And that bastard had hurt him. Scared him. Taken a piece of his innocence that he'd never get back. No amount of love I could give him would erase that moment. That terror. It was there and it would always be in his nightmares. In his thoughts. It would mold the man he would become and I hated the fact I wasn't able to save him from it.

I would blame myself for not moving faster. For waiting and being patient like the attorneys had suggested I do. I knew the day my father would start hitting him would come and I wanted to have him out of here before he did. But I hadn't managed it.

"You came! You didn't call this morning and I thought that you weren't coming." The joy and relief in his eyes almost put me on my knees.

"Didn't you talk to your mom yesterday?" I asked him. Hilda had said she would tell him I was coming. I had already assured him I would but I asked that she remind him. I knew his calls were monitored and I didn't want my father to be alerted that I'd spoken to Wills twice so soon. He'd get suspicious. I didn't need that. Not now.

He nodded. "She called but she didn't tell me. She said she was visiting you. But that's it."

He didn't ask if she'd come. He didn't ask if she was coming. He was six years old and he didn't care if his mother was coming to see him. I had asked her to come with me, but she'd gotten a call from her married boyfriend and left in tears. I wasn't sure if I would return to her at my place, or if she was left for Chicago.

"She was supposed to. I'm sorry. I should have called," I told him. He needed to be reassured. He didn't get that anywhere else in his world. Hilda should have thought of that. But she would rarely think beyond her needs and wants.

"Can I come to Savannah with you?" He asked me this a lot. He wanted to stay with me. My father never allowed it. He said I was too busy to fool with "the kid." And he'd said it in front of

Wills.

"Soon. I promise," I replied. "But today we are going to the M&M store to get you a large bag of the blue ones you love with whatever word you want on them this time. Then I thought we'd visit the zoo, and throw the football."

"I don't have a football," he said seriously.

"Oh, that's right. I forgot the part where we buy one at Nike Town," I added.

He was grinning now. He'd told me last time I visited that he didn't have a football and he wanted to learn to throw one.

"Can we leave now?" He wiggled to get down out of my arms.

"Absolutely. I need some of those yellow M&M's."

He smirked. At that moment, I saw myself. A picture from my youth. It was different now I knew. I wasn't imagining the similarities—they were there and they were real. He was my son.

"Yellow is a girl color," he told me as if I should know this.

"Like hell it is," I argued.

"You should get blue or green," he said with authority. "Even red is better than yellow."

"Don't bully me. I'll get pink if you do," I warned him.

His eyes went wide. "Really?"

"Hell, yeah, I will. Takes a real man to eat the pink ones," I told him.

He frowned. "You can't get the pink ones anywhere but at the M&M store. They don't even put those in the bag." He said this as if it was very important.

I shrugged. "Too bad."

"Do you think we can make it to the zoo to watch the Sea Lion's get fed?" He changed the subject once again.

"I'll check the time on my phone and we'll make sure to be

there for it."

"In the next couple months, they'll start eating more than normal. They do that to prepare for the winter. Makes them fatter and the fat makes them warmer."

I was impressed he knew that. "Did you learn about it in school?" I asked him.

"No, I read about it."

"Did you get a book about animals?" I asked him wondering who had bought it for him.

"I googled it," was his response.

"Would you like a book about animals?" I asked him since he was interested enough to Google it.

He nodded. "Yeah that would be cool."

I'd buy him every book they had at the store if he wanted them.

Chapter Twenty-Two
BEULAH

STONE DIDN'T COME back from Manhattan for the next two days, but he called often. His tone was different—happy almost.

Hilda hadn't returned. When or if she did, I was supposed to call Stone immediately. I wasn't sure I wanted to spend any time alone with her. But Stone did need her and I hoped she wasn't backing out on him. Having both biological parents would make the difference.

When I got home after seven and saw that Hilda's car wasn't back, I texted Stone to let him know there was still no sign of her. The coast was clear so I headed for the entrance. Before I could reach the door, Marty or Mack opened it and came walking out. The smile on his face and his wink when he saw me told me it was Mack.

"Hey, beautiful. Still alone up there?" he asked.

"Yes. Stone isn't back yet. He's spending time with his brother,"

I replied. It felt weird calling Wills his brother now. We'd decided it was best to continue as things were until this was handled.

He nodded his head toward the door. "Marty is making a mess which means it'll taste great. You're welcome to join. It's just us tonight."

I wondered where the others were. Especially since I knew they did indeed have a sex life with other occupants in the building.

"What happened to your usual dinner date?" I asked him.

He grinned. "Fight night on Pay Per View. She won't watch it. Hates the violence."

I had no idea what fight night was. I nodded anyway. "Thank you, but I ate with Geraldine. I knew I was coming home to an empty apartment."

"What happened to the hot ass cougar that was staying up there? I was enjoying her attempts to get me naked."

"Hilda?" I was surprised by his comment.

"I guess. She never told me her name. Mid-thirties maybe, but had some work done and looked younger. I can always tell though. The hands tell the age. You just have to pay attention. She was also horny as fuck—that makes her over thirty-five. I've found the ones who are panting with need are the ones whose man is too old to keep them sated."

That was more information than I needed. I didn't want to think about Hilda doing the same to Stone when I wasn't around.

"She's one of Stone's former stepmothers," I explained. I left out that she was Wills' mom. I don't know why but I didn't want to share that.

"Dayum, that must have been a good home life. Hot-ass, half-naked stepmothers walking around." Mack chuckled. "Anyway, if you change your mind, come eat. Door is always open."

Remembering that Hilda and Stone had been together once made me feel slightly crazy. I had been reading about my hormones today from the booklet that the doctor gave me. It had also suggested websites to visit for more information. I knew that my clingy, jealous emotions were normal. And that they would pass. I was ready for them to pass. I didn't like this at all. My eyes stung suddenly and I was on the verge of tears.

"Thanks." I quickly hurried past him embarrassed by my reaction to his words. I felt like a lunatic and if he saw me about to cry he'd probably think I was one too.

"You okay?" he called up after me as I ran up the stairs. He had walked back inside to check on me. Great.

"Yes, I'm fine." I tried my hardest to sound fine, but my voice cracked and I ran faster up the stairs needing to get away from him before I started crying and he could hear me.

Hiding that I was pregnant wasn't going to be the easiest thing I'd ever done. Especially if this was going to last a few weeks, possibly months. I needed to read more about it. There had to be a way to control my emotional swings better than I was.

Once I was inside the apartment I let the tears go and a sob broke free. Even as I cried I wasn't sure why I was crying exactly. Because once seven years ago Stone had had sex with Hilda? That even sounded ridiculous. Covering my face, I slid down the wall and cried. Might as well get it over.

I missed my mom. I could tell her. She'd know what I should do. She'd be there to answer all my questions.

I was alone. I couldn't tell Stone. He had too much to deal with and there was the chance he wouldn't want the baby. Not when he was fighting for the child he already had.

I was scared. What if I did something wrong? What if that

night of drinking had hurt the baby? What if I was a terrible mother?

The tears continued and so did my train of thought. I didn't fight it. I just let it go until there were no more tears and I was exhausted from the outburst. Once it was all dried up I sighed and stood. My body was weak and I started to go to the bedroom but stopped and went to the kitchen instead. I needed water.

Or did I need something more? Like milk? Was I drinking enough milk for the baby or did that matter when you were pregnant? Again more questions I had no one to ask. I started to get my phone and google it but decided I'd just drink the milk.

Taking the glass down I poured it halfway and then drank it before rinsing it and putting it in the dishwasher. I would need to go buy a book about this. One I could check when I had these questions.

Today was the first official day of my missed period. Tomorrow it will seem even more real. The child inside me only had me right now. I had to be sure to take care of it. Not harm it. I couldn't forget to eat. I also needed to exercise more. Maybe I should run with Fiona. Or would running make the baby fall out? That wasn't possible I didn't think.

I needed a "how to" book.

I would start walking for now. I could get up an hour earlier and walk every morning. And I would need to eat something first wouldn't I? Or would that make me vomit? Wasn't I supposed to be throwing up by now?

I had to stop thinking this through. Worry wasn't good either. The doctor had told me that much. Especially when I started asking a million questions.

A warm bath sounded good. But not too warm. Or did that

matter?

"UGH! I need an instruction manual!" I said out loud to no one. My voice echoed down the long hallway and I followed the lonely sound to Stone's bedroom. I wanted to be near him tonight. Sleeping in his room would help.

My phone rang and I saw his name on the screen. A smile instantly touched my lips. "Hello," I said feeling much better.

"Are you okay?" he asked not sounding equally happy.

"Yes, why?"

"Mack called. Said he thought he made you cry but he wasn't sure. He doesn't know what he said but you ran off with tears in your eyes. "

Crap. He'd seen me. I was going to be thought of as the crazy girlfriend.

"Oh, I'm fine. No tears I had just drank a lot of water and was in a hurry to get to the bathroom," I lied easily enough. It was a little scary how good I was at it.

Stone didn't respond right away. Maybe I wasn't as good at it as I thought.

"I'll be home in the morning," he said his tone still serious. "Or do you need me tonight? Is Heidi okay? Has Jasper contacted you?"

He hadn't bought the needing to pee thing. Well at least I sucked as a liar.

"I'm fine. Really."

"Call me if you need me. I love you," he said the last three words fiercely. As if he needed me to remember that.

"I love you too," I replied. And I did. But I wasn't sure our love was ready for what lay ahead.

Chapter Twenty-Three
STONE

BEFORE I LEFT today, I had been planning to confront my mother about my father. I wanted her to explain why we shared no DNA. After talking to Mack and hearing the uncertainty and emotion Beulah was trying so hard to hide on the phone last night, I knew I had to return home. There was no time to track down my mother. She'd lie to me anyway. Giving up the heir to the Richardson empire wasn't something she'd do without a fight.

The only way I could get home to Beulah before she woke up this morning was hire a private plane. Which I did. She was upset and I couldn't shake off feeling I was about to lose her. Even when I knew she wasn't the kind to run over something family issues. The bad feeling was still there in my gut. She was slipping away and I had to find a way to hold on to her.

Spending more time with her would be a start. I didn't know how I would manage that with what I was about to sail into. The steps to fight for custody of Wills were now in place. I had to be prepared to leave at a moment's notice. I had to be fully prepared for my father's fury and his counterattack.

Frustrated with my limited options, I unlocked the apartment door and went inside. It was three hours before Beulah had to get up. I didn't want to be the cause of her losing sleeping, but I also needed the reassurance of being beside her in bed holding her.

I locked the door behind me, dropped my keys on the table by the door and headed down the hallway. The bedroom that had been hers was dark and empty. That was reassuring. She hadn't slept in there since the other night when I wasn't here. She wasn't trying to distance herself from me. I wanted her in my bed when I wasn't there. I liked knowing she was near my things.

My bedroom door was closed. I opened it slowly and stepped inside. It was dark and it took me a moment for my eyes to adjust and see her sleeping in my bed. She was curled up on the side where I normally slept. She definitely wasn't trying to get away from me. She was getting as close to me while I was gone as she could.

I removed my shoes, stepped out of my jeans and took my shirt off. As quietly as I could I moved to the bed and eased in behind her. She'd wake up in a few hours and probably scream when she realized she wasn't alone. In her sleep, she sank back into my arms and made a pleased sound.

Inhaling, I let her sweet scent comfort me. She was here. In my home. With my things. She wasn't leaving me. My worries were probably caused from the stress I was under with getting custody of Wills. I'd never had someone that I was scared of losing. Now I had two. Beulah and Wills. When you live most of your life having loved only two people, it is hard to adjust to loving others. Not just loving them, but loving them more fiercely than you've ever loved anyone else.

It's fucking terrifying and makes you vulnerable. I didn't like feeling vulnerable, but I wouldn't have it any other way. Without the vulnerability, there was no Beulah. There was no Wills. I would take the weakness. Gladly.

"Is the baby okay?" she mumbled.

Frowning, I raised up on my elbow and looked down at her. She wasn't awake. Her eyes were still closed. What baby? Wills? He wasn't a baby anymore. I guess to her he was. They'd meet soon. Wills would love her.

"Yes, he's fine," I assured her although I was positive she was sleeping.

"Mmm," She snuggled closer to me.

I pressed a kiss to her temple and closed my eyes. I hadn't been tired on my way here. Now that I had her in my arms and knew that she was safe, sleep began to take me.

The dreams came quickly. I was working but living back at the house I had shared with my friends during college. They were there along with others I hadn't seen since graduation. It was a normal scene with drinking and gambling. I was standing back watching and saw Hilda walk inside with Wills beside her. That was out of place. She never came around and I hadn't seen Wills since Christmas. Frowning, I started walking toward her when Beulah walked in behind her. Her face was streaked with tears and her were eyes swollen and red. She had been crying.

Panic gripped me as a startled cry jerked me from my sleep and my eyes snapped back open.

Beulah was sitting up looking down at me with her hand over her mouth and her eyes wide.

"I'm sorry, I didn't mean to scream. I just woke up and someone was behind me. It scared me. Go back to sleep," she whispered after dropping her hand from her mouth.

I reached up and pulled her down to me with the hand she wasn't currently sitting on. She came down over me willingly. Her lips met mine softly and the dream was forgotten. I no longer remembered the exact specifics or where I had been in the dream. It wasn't important. This was.

Beulah shifted until half her body was covering mine. Her soft skin felt like silk. My hands slid under the T-shirt she was sleeping in and I found her naked underneath. I wasn't sleepy anymore.

"Go back to sleep," she said breaking the kiss.

"Don't want to," I replied and began kissing a trail down her neck and toward her collarbone.

"You got in late," she argued, but her voice hitched as I took a small bite of her neck.

"I got in about an hour ago," I told her.

"Stone! You need to get sleep," she said as her hands tried to push me away. I slid a hand between her legs and found her wet. She jerked against my hand and cried out softly.

"Let me decide what I need." I smiled at her response as I continued to tease her already aroused body.

Her breathing deepened and her head fell forward on my chest. Sounds similar to that of a kitten came from her as I ran a finger across her slit then slipped it inside her tight hole. Her vaginal walls squeezed it and my dick twitched in response. It wanted to be where my finger was. I didn't blame it.

Lifting a knee, I spread her legs and pulled her over me completely while moving her entrance to hoover over my now erect cock. "Sit on it," I demanded.

She was done arguing about my sleep. Her hands found my shoulders as she balanced her body then dropped her bottom until she found the connection we both were waiting for. I expected her to ease it in but she surprised me and dropped down hard on me taking it with one thrust.

"God!" she cried and her head was thrown back as if she'd been craving this for years.

"Take it," I told her.

She opened her eyes and looked down at me. Her lids were heavy and her mouth slightly open. Flushed cheeks and a touch of wildness was in her gaze. She liked the idea of being in control. I rarely gave her that when it came to sex, but seeing her above me like this was so damn exciting I couldn't figure out why.

My hands were under her shirt grasping her waist. She reached for the hem and pulled it up and over her head leaving her bare on top of me. Unable to look away I was entranced by the sight of her naked body as she began to bounce on my dick.

Each sway and jiggle of her breasts paired my visual stimulation with the feeling of my cock getting squeezed and soaked by her silken pussy. Thankful for the birth control, I groaned knowing she needed to get off soon because I was going to shoot a load in her real damn fast with her beautiful tits in front of me.

Her panting grew louder and her breasts bounced higher. Hair fell over her shoulders and brushed the nipples before she threw her head back once again. She was lost in the build toward her climax. Her vagina was quivering as she neared the summit.

I needed her to fucking hurry. I was almost there.

Using my fingers, I ran the pad of my thumb over her clit and she shouted out my name before she slammed down on me. I saw her body jerk and begin to tremble.

Taking her hips, I gripped them hard and held her there on me. "Fuck!" Lifting my hips, I kept my eyes locked on her and heard myself mumbling gibberish as I filled her with my own release. Her thighs were sweaty against mine as she squeezed and took it all. Every ounce. Her hair had fallen down to brush my chest as she gasped for breath. She let her head hang forward, spent.

My fears, concerns, and whatever reasons I felt I had to get back here to her were now eased. She didn't feel like a woman slipping away from me.

She climbed off me and bent down to press a kiss to my mouth. "That was a nice way to wake up." She grinned shyly.

"Hell yeah, it is. Want to go back to sleep and do it again before you have to get up?"

She giggled and walked toward the bathroom. I watched her go thinking this was going to be okay. I could keep it all handled. I didn't have to let go of one to have the other. She wanted me to get Wills too. She was on my side. My insecurities were deep rooted and I had to stop letting them get the best of me. Beulah was nothing like my mother.

Chapter Twenty-Four
BEULAH

SIX DAYS AFTER Stone's return, Hilda still hadn't come back. He wasn't talking about it, but I knew her not being here was concerning him. He needed Hilda to face the custody of Wills. She knew that. I hated to see the tension and stress in his eyes. The scowl that I caught him with when he was thinking made me worry about everything too. I knew he wasn't telling me all of it. I only got bits and pieces.

Hilda hadn't called or returned his calls. He had shared that with me last night. Preparing to fight this without her was his next step, but I suggested he fly to Chicago to talk to her. He didn't think it would help. She was only after whatever got her attention. This wasn't about Wills for her. She'd made that obvious with her actions.

Our sex wasn't hindered by any of this. Selfishly, I was thankful. I woke up several times about to orgasm. My body was doing crazy things. I wanted sex all the time. It was as if the simple act of walking stimulated me so much I began to ache for release. Stone was accommodating and didn't seem concerned with my new nymphomaniac tendencies. I knew they had to be caused by my pregnancy.

I'd enjoyed sex with him before. Loved it. But this was different. I just needed to get off. It sounded unromantic and honestly at times it was. Sex was all my body seemed to want. Not the sweetness that I had wanted before. I was aching to be used. My face flushed from even thinking about it.

Standing in the bathroom I stared at my body in the mirror. My breasts were tender. So much so that brushing against them made me tingle between my legs. That was new. They also ached from just being touched by a bra. I'd gone without one a couple days in a row thinking it would help but all it had really done was stimulated me further from my shirt constantly teasing them.

I squeezed my legs together and the tenderness down there wasn't just because I was constantly asking to be fucked, but because it felt more sensitive too. I had googled both things and apparently it was normal and expected. Most men enjoyed this part of the pregnancy with their wives or girlfriends. Stone didn't even realize he was enjoying that exactly. To him we were just going at it like maniacs because we could.

My hips weren't wider and my stomach was still flat. I was one week past my expected period. I'd read that it meant I was five weeks pregnant. My body didn't feel different except for the constant state of horniness. I wasn't getting sick. I wasn't having food cravings.

Suddenly, Stone was yelling at someone. I grabbed my jeans and T-shirt and dressed quickly before running to see what was happening. By the time I got the bedroom door open, Stone was yelling again but I couldn't hear anyone else.

I followed the sound of his voice to the kitchen where he was standing with his phone to hi ear. His face was red and his furious glare was directed at the wall while the person on the other end of the call continued to talk to him. It wasn't helping. They were only making him angrier.

"How could you?" He grabbed a chair from the kitchen table and hurling it against the wall. There were obvious marks on the wall now and a small dent while the chair lay with a broken leg on the ground. I jumped back unsure if I should try to calm him or move to another room for protection.

"Wills isn't his son! You crazy ass bitch!!!"

I started to leave the room and to wait in the living room. That caused me to pause. The phone call was about Wills. Hilda had done something. From the sounds of it, that something was terrible.

"I want him!" was his response to whatever was said on the other end.

As he listened his breathing was fast, his face so bent with rage I was nervous. But I didn't leave the room. I waited for him to finish the call. He was facing yet another obstacle. One that was caused by Wills' mother.

"Fine," his voice was eerily calm now—low and cold with zero emotion. His calmness was scarier than the shouting had been. "You do what you need to. Find your happiness. I will finish this." He ended the call and his phone stayed there tightly in his grasp as he breathed heavily through his nose.

I didn't move. He didn't speak and the time ticked by. Although I wanted to go to him and hold him. I wanted to comfort him. I didn't think would me near him at the moment. He needed space. And that meant from me too.

He hadn't seen or heard from Wills since last week. He'd tried to call, but the nanny always said Wills was unavailable or not home. Stone didn't want to push too hard for fear of drawing his father's attention. As evidenced by his reaction to Hilda's phone call, today something more had happened. Stone seemed determined and broken at the same time. Whatever Hilda had done it didn't change that Wills was Stone's biological son.

"The senator's wife found out about Hilda. That's why she came here. Not for Wills. The Senator has begged her to come back and he's put her up in fucking Malibu. She's in California. She's not helping me. Not helping her son. She said it would draw unwanted attention to her that her precious senator doesn't want. And if I press this further she's going to give up all rights to Wills. Allow the motherfucker sole custody and she'll live like a wealthy mistress."

His voice wasn't angry now, it was empty. Hollow. His pain was apparent, but it was the lack of any emotion as he said the words that were so haunting. I didn't believe he was giving up but his words sounded defeated.

"He doesn't even like her. Wills. He doesn't like Hilda. He wants to like her. I think he's conflicted." Stone laughed hard but there was no humor. "Fucking conflicted about how he feels about his mother and he is six years old. Jesus, he's gonna be as screwed up as I am. The harder I fight to stop this, the worse it gets. I get a break and then I'm knocked back several feet."

I didn't move. I wanted to. God, I wanted to go to him so bad. But I stayed put. He was dealing with it all by talking about it out loud. Telling me was his way of dealing. He hadn't even looked at me yet. His focus was still on the wall he had damaged in front of him.

He ran a hand through his hair and sighed. "I wasn't meant to have children. I never wanted them. How the fuck am I expected to be a father to a boy when I have no model to follow? Why didn't I realize I had zero ability at parenting when I was fifteen years old? Teenage boys should be fucking locked away until they can think with something other than their dicks."

My heart slowly sank even further as he went on about how he wasn't meant to be a father. How he couldn't handle the responsibility. How he would have no idea how to even do it right. He believed everything he was saying. The way the words seemed to lash out and cut him as they came out of his mouth made it very clear he didn't want them to be true, but he believed they were.

"I am not a father. No kid deserves this." He pointed at himself. "It's why I wanted you on birth control. I fucked up a few times, but fate didn't make the same mistake again with me. Thankfully, we didn't create a life. I couldn't deal with that. Especially now." He looked at me. His eyes were so dark and lost. The heartache he'd lived through since his childhood clear in his blue depths. As he bared his soul to me, shared all the pain, I found a way to keep from shattering. I held myself together and I found strength I didn't know I possessed as I listened to him.

He didn't want the life growing inside me. He couldn't deal with fatherhood. He had called getting pregnant a mistake. He didn't realize it but he had. And although I disagreed with him. I knew the man he was. I knew he would be an excellent father. What mattered was he didn't think that. And he didn't want to be a father. He firmly believed it was impossible for him to be a good parent.

The urge to cover my stomach with both hands to protect

the baby from his words was strong, but I resisted. Stone couldn't know. Mentally, he wasn't prepared right now. He had Wills to focus on and it was clearly wearing him down. His stress level was at its peak.

And he didn't want a child, not even with me. My heart was destroyed, but I wouldn't break. I couldn't because it wasn't only me anymore. I had someone besides Heidi that would need me. I would be all this child had. I'd do anything, absolutely anything to make sure my baby was cared for.

Wills didn't have a mother to do that for him. If Stone didn't fight for him, no one would. But Stone didn't want to be a father. He was doing trying to get custody of Wills because he had no choice. This baby, my baby, wouldn't be a burden. It would be a blessing. What Stone had called a mistake, I would raise to believe they were a special gift from God. Chosen by my mother to complete me and bring me joy. I'd keep my heartache and pain hidden.

"I'll have to fly back to Manhattan. I need to regroup with my attorneys and decide what to do now. I should also check in on Wills to see if he's okay."

I simply nodded my head. Yes, he needed to go. And so did I.

He walked over and I stood in front of me. The urge to run to him and hold him in my arms was no longer there. That emotion, those feelings had somehow vanished or were simply shut off by his words. His arms wrapped around me and I hugged him back. My mind told me not to allow this to affect me while my heart hurt so badly it was hard to breathe. The two weren't on the same page.

I didn't stop loving him because he didn't want a child. Not wanting a child simply made it impossible for me to stay with him. Maybe one day I wouldn't love him. Maybe watching our child grow up would remind me of what could have been. Had he been stronger. Had he wanted us.

Chapter Twenty-Five
STONE

BEULAH HAD WITHDRAWN again. I had fought against leaving. Then I'd considered calling Gerry and seeing if Beulah could take the week off so she could fly to New York with me. Gerry would have let her of course, but Beulah wouldn't have been happy with me. She'd be worried about leaving her. I would have had a fight on my hands.

Finally, I decided that I was being paranoid. All this shit I was dealing with had to be messing with my head. Beulah had been more than affectionate all week. We'd fucked all over every inch of the house. This morning she'd seen me upset and ranting and it had startled her. She hadn't ever seen that side of me.

Leaving was no longer an option—I had to go. My first stop would be to check in on Wills since he hadn't been available for phone calls all week. Then I was making a trip to my mother's house. She needed to answer some questions for me. I would have to work to get the truth but I had time. Without her answers, I couldn't move forward with my life. And now that Hilda was no longer fighting for Wills, I had more work on my hands.

I texted Beulah as soon as I landed at JFK Airport, but she hadn't responded and it had been over an hour. I arrived to check on Wills and battled if I should call her or check on Wills first. I decided she could be busy and I would give her more time. If she hadn't responded in a couple hours I would call.

When I reached the front door and rang the bell, I expected the door to open within seconds like it always did. My father's staff had always been overly efficient. If they weren't he fired them.

However, after a couple of minutes I was still standing outside. I rang again and waited. Time ticked slowly and no one came to the door. This wasn't normal. It was so abnormal that I began to grow worried. I pulled my phone back out of my pocket and called the number that would reach Wills nanny.

It rang and then went to a voicemail.

I called the main house line.

Again I got voicemail.

As much as I didn't want to, I called my father. This was his house and no one was answering the door or phone, and that was so out of character that there was no reasonable explanation for it. My worry was escalating to fear as my stomach roiled. Wills hadn't been available all week. But at least I had spoken to the Nanny.

This silence was different.

My father's voicemail was the last warning flag I needed. There was something off. This sudden cut of communication wasn't just a coincidence. They weren't all busy. This had been planned. Wills inability to talk to me all week now felt more suspicious than understandable.

I walked away from the house as I dialed my father's office.

He may not be answering but I knew that Richardson Enterprises would be open for business.

"Good Afternoon, Richardson Enterprises. How can I direct your call?" It was Margaret. She was thirty-seven, divorced, had three kids, and was sleeping with Harold from marketing. Harold was married and thirty years old, no kids. I knew my father's employees. I made it point to know everything about them. Something he never did and that I'd hoped would help me one day.

"Hello, Margaret. It's Winston. How are you today?"

"Oh, hello Winston. I'm doing great. Thank you," the smile in her tone was always flirty. Even though she was fifteen years older than me and currently involved in an affair. She liked the attention from men.

"How did Bart's tennis match go?" I asked remembering she had mentioned her oldest son Bart had a tennis tournament when I had spoken with her last week while visiting the office.

"He was amazing. The kid is going to be a star!" she bragged.

"I'm sure he will be. Sure sounds like it." I wasn't sure I believed her. With the way she was handling her personal life, that kid had more drama coming in his future. That would either send him off the tracks or make him want more drama. "Could you put me through to my father, please?"

She paused. "Oh, I would. But he's in Europe. I assumed you knew."

Europe? "No, he didn't mention it. Where in Europe?"

I heard her shuffling around and her voice sounded muffled as if she were covering something up. "Switzerland, I think. He's taken Wills to get settled into the boarding school."

He had Wills in Switzerland to enroll in a boarding school. He was six years old. Who the fuck sent a six-year-old to boarding school? "Are you sure?" I asked her still thinking there had to be some miscommunication.

"Yes. I know," she whispered. "I didn't think it was even legal to send a six-year-old off like that. But he did. I thought you knew. Wills' mother knew. She sent over the signed paperwork."

Hilda knew. She fucking knew and didn't tell me.

I couldn't say anymore. I was in shock. There was nothing the man could do to surprise me, but Hilda had let this happen? No concern at all for Wills?

"Thank you." I forced out the words before ending the call.

I wanted to hit something or to throw the man I had believed was my father against a wall over and over. I wanted to make him beg for compassion. None of that would help Wills now. I had to take a deep breath and not think about how scared he had to be right now. Not worry about his safety where he was. If I did I would go crazy. Wills needed me to be smart and to move quickly.

I never imagined taking my time would lead to this. I was trying to be safe. Make sure when I went after custody of my son that I had the power to win. It wasn't easy to go up against a man as powerful as Richardson. But now it was time to move. To strike. To fucking get my son back in the United States.

Driving toward my lawyer's firm I called and let them know I was on my way and that

there was a development that would require immediate action. I'd tell them more when I arrived. While I was on the phone with my counsel, I that about calling Beulah back. Hearing her voice and talking to her about what had happened would help me focus. Now more than anything I wished I had brought her with me. I needed her. Gerry would have understood. I'd talk to her and then tell Gerry. I wanted Beulah here with me.

The phone rang and like all the other damn numbers I had called there was no answer. Slamming my phone down in the passenger seat I focused on the road and went over all my options to get Wills back. Beulah would call me back soon. She wasn't my father. There was no secret there. Nothing she was hiding. Nothing I had to fear.

Once I had her here with me I could focus more on the situation instead of worrying about her. Wills was my son and having Beulah as a part of his life now was important. For all three of us. Wills was going to need Beulah just as much as I did.

I fiddled with my phone as it sat in the passenger seat. I thought of calling Gerry's now, but I had a meeting to get to. I would call after. By the time I went to bed tonight, Beulah would be on a plane headed here.

Chapter Twenty-Six

BEULAH

ALTHOUGH HE WAS miles away, I still felt time closing in on me.

Stone had texted and called today. Both times I hadn't been able to respond. Speaking to him and hearing his voice was too much. Kissing him goodbye knowing it was the last time I'd kiss him crippled me emotionally. I'd been on the verge of tears all day. More than once I had found myself thanking Geraldine for the job and all she'd done for me. How her friendship meant so much and how I would always cherish our memories forever. I hadn't been able to tell her I was leaving because doing so would mean I'd have to tell her why.

For the child growing inside me, I couldn't do it. I had someone else to protect now. This baby would come first for the rest of my life. It wasn't something I had to remind myself of, it just came naturally. Knowing that Stone didn't want the baby made me feel even more fiercely protective. As if I could be enough for both parents.

If I told Geraldine, she'd have to tell Stone. Instead I made our last day count. I spent time doing all the things I had been wanting to get to, I made her favorite meals and we sat outside like she loved to do. I listened to her stories and laughed enjoying the moment. This would be my last memory with her and I soaked it all in.

Once she went upstairs for a nap, I made extra meals and placed them in the fridge. She would be okay until Stone got back. When I left her house. I went to see Heidi. It was unexpected and much later than I had ever visited before.

Heidi had been my world for so long. She'd been my number one priority. Now she was safe. Taken care of. I'd have to one day make sure Stone was paid back for her care to protect. Right now I had no other option. I'd have to owe him.

Leaving town meant leaving Heidi here. I would come back for her when I could. I would visit her but not as often as I did now. She was happy with her friends and her home. Taking her from all that was unfair especially when I wasn't able to make sure she had proper care and food. This was where she would be safest.

When Heidi came out of her room and saw me walking down the hall, she'd beamed at me and ran to hug me fiercely. I held onto her tightly. Trying not to cry. She wouldn't understand. I knew that. But I had to tell her. She was the one person I couldn't leave without telling her why. She depended on me. And I never wanted her to think I was gone forever like Mom was.

"Beulah, you surprised me!" she said loudly with such happiness in her voice. This was going to be difficult.

"I wanted to see you," I told her and kissed her cheek.

"I made a pillowcase today! Come see!" she grabbed my hand

and pulled me to her room.

I went, thankful that we were going to be in her room alone. No one to hear me or hear Heidi's questions. She ran over to her bed and took a pillow off of it. It was covered in painted flowers. Yellow daisies like the ones our mother loved so much. I knew she remembered her. My eyes stung as I saw that memory showing through on the pillow she had painted. I didn't want her to think I was going away like our mother had. She needed to know I would always be here. Explaining that to her seemed so difficult. Her capability of understanding the difference wasn't exactly clear. I wasn't sure what all Heidi did or didn't completely understand. Sometimes I thought I knew and other times I wondered if she figured out more than I realized or gave her credit for.

"It's beautiful," I assured her as I touched the pretty yellow flowers.

"I learned to sew on a machine. They taught us and it was fun." Her excitement was contagious.

Another reason I loved it here. It wasn't just a care facility. They taught Heidi things I never could. They made her feel as if she were capable of so much more than the world let her believe she was.

"You will have to teach me one day," I told her. "I would love to know how to sew."

Heidi nodded enthusiastically. "May sewed a skirt. It's pink and has white hearts. It's too big for her, but Tammy said that she could wear it."

Tammy was one of the nurses. And I had no doubt Tammy would wear the skirt proudly. May would be so pleased and the others would be impressed. This place provided Heidi with the family she needed and the kind I couldn't give her. I was struggling to find my way in the world and now I was going to have to build a life to bring a child into. A life where I could support the child and give it all my mother had given us.

"Heidi, I need to talk to you about something. It's a secret. Something I can only tell you and no one else can know. Do you understand?" I wasn't sure this was the way to tell her, but I knew my time was limited. I had to make a move tonight. Talking to Heidi was the only thing I absolutely had to do other than pick my things up from Stone's.

She nodded and a frown creased her brow. "I can keep a secret. I promise."

I knew she'd try very hard to never tell what I was about to tell her. But I also knew it was going to be hard for her to accept or understand. Leaving her alone for a while wasn't something she had ever dealt with. I didn't know if she could accept what I was going to share with her.

I put my hand on my stomach and looked at her. I thought about how Mom would tell her this. How she would explain to Heidi that I had no other choice. Channeling the woman who had loved us and raised us, I took a deep breath and held her gaze. "Inside my stomach is a baby. It's growing. And my stomach will get big and the baby will be born. Do you understand that?" I paused to give her a moment to take that in. Digest it. Figure out how that affected her. What it meant for her.

Her eyes grew wide and she nodded slowly. "You're going to be a mommy."

Her simple words were so powerful. I was going to be someone's mother. I was going to be the person they relied on to live. Me. I swallowed the fear clawing at my throat and threatening to stop my oxygen flow.

She didn't ask who the daddy was. Simply because she had never seen a father in our life. There was no daddy. She didn't know there was a man required for creating a baby. Instead, she asked, "Is it a boy or girl baby?" The excitement in her voice was evident.

"I don't know yet. I won't know for a long time still." A few months was forever to Heidi. Which was why telling her I had to go away was so hard. I wouldn't stay away for months at a time. I knew I couldn't do that to her. But making it back here was going to be hard. Once a month was all I could promise right now. Until I knew more about where I was going to live and work.

"Will I be able to hold it?" She was still wide-eyed with amazement.

"Yes. You'll be the best aunt in the world."

She slapped a hand over her mouth as if I had just told her the most fantastic news she'd ever heard. I waited for her to put her thoughts into words. "I'm going to be an aunt?" she whispered as if that was the ultimate secret.

I nodded. "The only aunt this baby will have," I told her.

We didn't have aunts. But Heidi knew what they were because she had friends here who had aunts. She had also watched enough television to understand what an aunt was.

"Ohmygod!" she squealed and clapped her hands rapidly while jumping up and down.

Again, I fought back tears. Because as happy as she was now I still hadn't told her what all this meant for us. How it would change her routine. How I wouldn't be here as much. How once again, she would have to adjust to change.

She threw her arms around me and hugged me tightly. "I will be the best aunt ever," she promised.

I had no doubt that she would. I held her to me and closed my eyes tightly fighting back emotion. My entire life I had protected her the best I could. Been there for her, loved her, and worried about her. She'd been my ultimate source of joy. Now, I was going to leave her. Put time and space between us while my first priority became someone new.

"I know you will," I replied. "But I need to tell you something else. Something that has to happen because of the baby inside me. It won't be forever, but for a time. It will change things and it won't be easy. It will make you sad, it will make me sad," I stopped and studied her a moment. I tried to decide what she understood. Her eyes were wide as she waited for me to tell her more. There was so much trust there. Her world was safe. She didn't understand the pain, sorrow, or fear that was just outside.

I was so very thankful for that.

"I need to take care of the baby and to do that I have to move to find a new house and a new job. I won't live close to here. I can't stay close and take care of the baby. There is someone who doesn't want me to have this baby. I need to keep the baby safe from them. I will come back once a month and see you. I'll bring cookies and I will stay the day. It won't be forever but for a while. Until I can figure out something else. For now, I need to find a place in another town." I stopped afraid I had said too much. More than she would understand.

She didn't reply right away. We stood there still holding onto each other but we did it in silence. I watched her expression change and I fought against the urge to say more. Try harder to explain. I knew she needed time to let this sink in and to work through it and figure it out. Hopefully she could accept this huge change.

"Will you and the baby be safe if you leave?" she asked me. Her question in a quiet voice but the sincerity and concern there was heartbreaking. I never wanted to cause Heidi to worry. I wanted her to live in happiness.

"Yes. I will find a place that we will be safe."

She frowned. "I want you to both be safe."

I squeezed her tightly in a hug. "I will make sure that we are."

"Promise?"

"Yes, I promise," I replied my eyes full of tears and slowly beginning to trickle down my cheeks. "And I will be back here to see you every chance I get."

"I like pink," she said.

"I will bring pink cookies and cupcakes," I assured her.

"No. I like to make pink blankets. I like pink clothes. I want the baby to be a girl."

A small laugh escaped me, drowning the sadness that was weighing on me. Only Heidi could do that when I was so low. "Maybe it will be. Just for you."

She didn't reply right away and I didn't push for more. This was going smoother than I expected. My heart was breaking. I was so proud of her it was also bursting.

"If it's a boy I will learn to love blue," she finally said after several moments.

I didn't reply. I was too choked up to say anything. Instead, I held her. My only family. All I had in this world. My special gift in life. My sister.

Chapter Twenty-Seven
STONE

I DROPPED THE phone in my hand as the call ended. Deep down I knew she was gone. Believing it was hard to accept. Unanswered questions hung in the balance and I knew I may never get to ask them. Gerry hadn't known much. She said that yesterday Beulah had been different. Sad, very grateful, and scared. When she hadn't shown up this morning, Gerry wasn't surprised. She'd waited until after lunch to call me.

It had been the day after my ninth birthday when my father had come to tell me my mother wouldn't be stopping by to visit again. She'd left to move to France with her new fiancé and wouldn't be back. He hadn't reassured me she would call or that she might miss me. He hadn't explained why I had heard nothing from her on my birthday. And when I had teared up from the feeling of abandonment he had slapped me across the face and told me to grow the fuck up. A man didn't cry. He was tough and lived his life at his own pace. A woman would always leave you and there would be plenty waiting to take her place.

I had been a child and none of that made sense at the time. The mark left by his hand, however, left an impact. It was the last time I had cried. Even alone at night when I felt as if there was no one who cared. Even knowing that I was unwanted and I had no purpose in life, I didn't cry. Because deep down I'd wanted to make that bastard proud of me. It had taken much more emotional abuse and neglect to finally destroy that desire. The day he held my son in his arms and told me that real men built their army of sons one woman at a time, I decided I wanted nothing to do with him. He wasn't anything I strived to be and became everything I fought against becoming.

Trusting anyone enough to love them had been so damn impossible for me that I'd almost lost Beulah. Then when I gave in to what I so clearly wanted and let myself love her, she left me when I need her the most—just like my mother had.

I didn't blame her. I was the common denominator. I was the one that they so easily ran from. What was it that was so wrong with me that sent them away? What did I lack that made me unworthy of their love? Was I more damaged than I realized? And if Beulah couldn't love me, if she couldn't stay, then was I good enough to raise Wills? Would I ruin him even more than my father had ruined me? Or had I become my father and not realized it.

I wanted to hate Beulah for leaving me.

I wanted to curse her name and then forget she existed.

I could do neither. I also couldn't find some female to fill the emptiness she left behind. Beulah had been special, unique. She'd claimed my fucking heart the moment I saw her which was stupid and naïve but it'd happened none the less. Yet something in me had turned her away and sent her running.

First, I had to rescue my son. He was innocent and he needed me. No one else did but Wills. And by God I wouldn't let that boy down. I'd fight until I had no fight left. He'd know I wanted him. He would know he was loved. I'd make sure if I did everything in this world to be everything that he ever needed.

As for Beulah, I'd return to Savannah when I could. She'd stay close because of Heidi. Finding her wouldn't be impossible. Then I'd make her tell me why she left me. She could tell me why women turned away from me and why she couldn't love me.

After I knew that, I would let her go. Free her. Move on with my life. But I'd never forget her. I'd always be marked by her. She'd claimed a part of me I wouldn't get back. And I didn't want to. And although she didn't want me and I wasn't enough, I would be there near her. Never leaving her side completely. Giving me hope there might be a time when I would smile again.

She was a light in a time I thought my world would be forever dark. I saw my life being void of real love until she stole my heart with a glance. Nothing more.

Moving on in life after you have loved a woman like Beulah seemed impossible. Accepting that you would always love her and that she would always be there as a silent part of you, made it easier to keep going. It was all I had left.

I would fight for my son. I wouldn't let him down. Then I would make a life for us. One where he understood security and love. My memories of Beulah would always be there—she couldn't take away.

I'd tried twice more to call her phone, but all I got was the voicemail. Finally, around three I got a call from Fiona. She never called me. I knew when her name appeared on my screen this was about Beulah. I stood up and walked out of the conference room that was filled with my team of lawyers and answered the called.

"She left last night," Fiona said after I said hello. "I thought about calling then but she said some things that kept me from it. I wasn't going to tell you anything. However, I like Beulah and after thinking about it all day and worrying about her, I decided I'd call you. She's alone. She's left town and she's the most fucking naïve human on the planet. Are you coming back to get her?"

She was annoyed but there was true concern in her tone. I didn't like that Beulah had left at night either. Where had she gone? It wasn't safe for her to be driving around at night alone. "I can't come back. I have to deal with something here. I didn't ask her to leave. She ran without saying anything to me." I said this to Fiona but I was also saying it for my benefit. Reminding myself that I wasn't available to drop it all and run after her.

"She's alone out there. I got no fucking sleep because of it," Fiona snapped.

"I didn't ask her to leave. She knows what I am dealing with. She knows I can't leave this. She's a grown ass woman and I can't force her to be safe." Saying the words didn't make me feel any better. If she was in danger, I'd never move on in life. It would kill me. But what the hell was I supposed to do? Wills was only a child.

"Actions speak louder than words." Fiona's annoyed tone only made me angrier.

"I have done all I could to protect her from the first moment I met her. I busted my ass to give her all she needed. Security, a home, and my motherfucking heart. Right now, I have a kid who needs me. One who has no power to take care of himself. I can't abandon him because a woman has decided to run off and leave behind all the security I provided for her. If she doesn't want me I can't force her to." After saying the words I ended the call.

Speaking to Fiona had only made me angrier.

Beulah was out there alone. I didn't know where she was or why she left. She had to be close by because of Heidi, but Savannah alone at night wasn't safe either. I tried like hell to shake off the fear. I told myself I didn't care.

Nothing worked.

I called her number as I stood outside the conference room. It rang until voicemail picked it up. My heart pounded in my chest and the anxiety that her safety was now a serious issue grew until I did the last thing I expected to ever do.

I scrolled down my contact list until I found Jasper's name. I didn't take time to think it through because I didn't have the time. I only knew that he loved her too.

"Yeah," he replied after four rings. His tone said he knew who this was and he wasn't interested in talking to me. I expected this.

"Beulah is gone. I'm in Manhattan and I can't leave. She's left me. She's without anyone." I stopped before I told him more. My secret had to remain one until time to fight for my son.

"I expected her to leave eventually. You can't be what she needs. It's not your nature."

His elitist tone made my jaw clench tightly and my knuckles turn white but I took it. She needed me to. She needed someone to help her. And he was the only someone I knew who would do it. No matter what kind of fight she put up.

"Will you find her? Help her? Please?" I didn't care that I sounded as if I were pleading because I was.

"Why me?"

"Because I believe you really loved her."

"I still do."

I closed my eyes tightly fighting back my stupid jealousy.

"Then please, Jasper. Find her and make sure she's safe."

"I'll go. Because of Beulah. Not because of you." That was why I had asked him. I knew he loved her. Because once you love Beulah it's impossible to forget. To let go.

"That's why I asked," I replied.

Jasper ended the call and I sat there staring at the wall in front of me. I had no way of knowing when and if he ever found her. I would never know if she was safe. And then there was the sick fear that she'd remember why she loved him. That she would miss what she had with him. She would compare what we had and it wouldn't be enough. She'd forget the reasons why it was wrong and she'd love him anyway. And she'd be gone forever.

Losing her was my fear from the beginning. To protect her, I had sent the one man to find her that could take her from me. Jasper could show her everything she was missing. But calling him was the only thing that made sense. Knowing she was safe and that she had a place to sleep was more important than not having her love. If I had to live without her, I would manage. But I couldn't live knowing she'd needed saving and I had done nothing. This was all I could do right now. And I had to trust that I'd made the right decision—the one that would take care of her. The one that would assure she was safe until I could return and find out if there was a chance for us.

Chapter Twenty-Eight
BEULAH

IF IT WASN'T for Heidi I would turn my phone off. Seeing Stone's name on the screen had hurt, but he stopped calling me yesterday. It hurt that he was giving up so quickly. I shook my head frustrated at my train of thought. It was better that Stone was letting me go. If he knew about the baby he'd leave me anyway. I wasn't going to be a burden to him and neither was my baby.

Fiona had also called several times yesterday and today. I felt guilty not answering her. She was worried when I left the other night. Eventually, I had told her it wasn't just me I had to take care of, she'd stopped trying to talk me into staying. When she paused to think that through, I left.

My phone started ringing once again and I glanced down to see Jasper's name. That had surprised me.

I turned my attention back to the interstate in front of me. I'd driven to Jacksonville, Florida the first night, finally pulling into a rest area with twenty-four-hour security to sleep in my car.

Even with the security I had locked the doors and climbed into the back seat and covered my entire body.

I had slept seven hours with no interruptions. When the sun came up and the car began to get warm even with the windows cracked I woke up and used that day to explore the city. I wanted to figure out if this could be my new home.

Unfortunately, the city was huge and everywhere I went I felt unsafe. It was also too close to Savannah. After a day of studying the area, I went back to the same rest area and slept. This morning started my journey to I had no idea where. I got back on the road this morning had decided to turn west instead of continuing my southward path. I'd glanced at a map on my phone and saw that once I made it out of Florida on this interstate I would enter Alabama. Using gas meant I would be spending money, and the further I got from Heidi the more money I would spend to get back to her. I started looking at every city I passed wondering if this would be the one I where I'd be happy to live.

My phone made an odd sound and I checked it to find out what it was doing, but nothing looked out of the ordinary. The sign ahead said Tallahassee exits were coming up and I'd heard of Tallahassee. I decided to stop and get food to stop my stomach from growling.

I could Google Tallahassee to figure out if this could be a place where I found a home, a job, and would raise my child. So far, I had spent fifty dollars on gas and my tank was almost at a fourth of a tank. I had to be careful not to get much further away from Heidi.

Although she'd handled my having to leave because of the baby much better than I expected I could see the uncertainty and sadness in her eyes when we said our goodbyes. She was scared and

I hated knowing I was leaving her. I would make it a point to visit more than once a month. Thinking about that made Tallahassee seem ideal as I planned my next step.

I pulled into the parking lot of a fast food chicken place and found a spot to park. My guilt over not answering Fiona was bothering me. I had a lot of guilt right now, I could at least alleviate that one.

I sent Fiona a text to reassure her I was safe and that I was where I had intended to stay. I thanked her for her friendship and added that I would miss all of them and hoped to one day see them again. Then I sent it. Feeling better about one person in my life, I put my phone down and reached into my purse to see how much cash I had. I was on a budget and normally food wasn't something I would take into such careful consideration. I had to eat well because I wasn't just eating for me. A candy bar and bottle of water wasn't going to be a meal option now.

The money in my bank account was plenty to rent a small affordable studio apartment, pay for the utilities to be turned on and to buy food. That would only last two months at most. I had to find a job immediately. A job where I could work until I gave birth. If I could get a job with health insurance that would be even better, but I wasn't going to get my hopes up. I knew I could qualify for state aid.

Taking out five dollars from my cash I got out of the car and walked inside to use the restroom and order myself some breakfast. The place was busy but it was one of the more popular fast food restaurants near the exit. I saw a mother with a baby on her hip and a toddler beside her holding his father's hand. They were discussing what the kids wanted to eat. It looked easy. Or they made it look easy. Would it be so easy when it was just me standing there with my baby? No man to help carry the tray or hold the child while I went to the restroom. Little things like that. My mother had done it. But I couldn't remember if it had been tough on her then. When we'd been little like that.

The line to the toilets wasn't bad and I watched as a mother changed a diaper and another helped her toddler wash her hands. With each baby and child I saw I began to imagine my baby and how it would look. Through all the anxiety and worry there was excitement. I smiled as I finished up in there and followed a mom with a baby out back into the busy dining room.

Standing in line I had time to plan out what I would order using my five dollars efficiently. Grilled chicken and fresh apples with a glass of water was just under my budget. It was also the healthiest option I could find on the menu. I got it to go and headed back out to the parking lot. Eating in the peace of my car would be easier than finding a table in that crowd. However, I only took a few steps in the direction of my car and when my eyes focused and I saw the figure standing there. It was a man leaning against my car with serious expression. I blinked several times to see if I was seeing things. But even with the morning sun in my eyes it was clearly Jasper Van Allan standing next to my car.

I didn't move. How did he find me here? Why did he come looking for me? All these questions ran through my head as I stared at him. He didn't move, he continued to watch me. I didn't want him here. I had too much to deal with and Jasper was one added problem. He couldn't find out about my baby. He couldn't find out why I had left and I wasn't telling him anything.

I walked to my care to confront him. I had no choice if I wanted in my car. This would ruin my quiet meal. My mind raced with every different scenario that would have led him here to me.

None of it made sense. I hadn't told a soul where I was going. I hadn't even known where I was going.

"Surprise," he said with a small smile tugging at his lips when I reached him. All I could do was stand there staring at him. I didn't have anything to say to him. The last time I had seen Jasper he'd intentionally hurt Stone. He'd shown how cruel and hateful he could be. I wouldn't ever forget that.

"Say something, Beulah. Glaring at me will get us nowhere." He sounded amused. I wasn't amused. Not in the least.

"Why are you here?" I asked. He wanted me to say something so there it was.

"To find you. I would have thought that was obvious."

I looked around the parking lot and back at him. "I'm in Tallahassee Florida, Jasper. No one knows where I am. I left without a word on purpose. So no, that isn't obvious. We haven't spoken since you so cruelly slashed your best friend with information you really didn't know for sure in hopes of turning me against him. My question is, why are you here? I didn't ask you to come nor do I want you here."

He winced. "Ouch. When did you get mean?"

"The truth sometimes hurts. Doesn't make me mean. Makes me honest," I shot back at him.

He lifted his left shoulder with a small shrug then nodded. "You're right. What I did was an asshole thing to do. But loving someone can make you do insane shit when you've lost them and can't find a way to live without them."

I sighed. He was back to the loving me thing. Although it had only been a few months ago that I fell in love with Jasper for a short brief fairytale romance, it seemed like another lifetime. It was all before I knew him, really. Before I knew the lies, the secrets, and it was before I knew Stone. Stone had been a mystery. After I got to know him, even his smile could make everything that was wrong in my world right. It was before I knew what it meant to truly give your heart completely to someone else.

"Why are you here?" I repeated instead of talking about the past. It needed to say there. Forgotten.

He dropped his hands from the crossed position over his chest. "Because you ran. You're alone. And I . . . we want you safe."

We? I frowned. "Who is we?"

His right eyebrow lifted as if I had just asked a stupid question. "You know who."

I waited a moment for him to clarify then my silly heart sped up as I said his name "Stone?"

Jasper nodded.

"Stone sent *you?*" I asked finding that hard to believe.

He winced again. "Damn you're trying to kill me. Why is that so hard to believe?"

"Oh, I don't know. Maybe because the last time we were all together you took his loyalty, friendship and a lifetime of trust and threw it in his face. You turned on him, abandoned him like every other person in his life except Gerry. You were his family and you tossed that away. After all he'd done for you." My voice gradually got louder as I spoke. I was starting to yell and snapped my mouth closed. I wasn't going to fight with him in a parking lot. Drawing attention was the last thing I needed.

Jasper didn't respond right away. He was silent. There was regret looming in his eyes. It was clear that he wished he hadn't done it. That helped my anger cool. Maybe he wasn't just like his mother after all. He felt remorse. He saw his faults and wanted to change them. Portia could not.

"I'll never forgive myself for what I did. I let my insanity when it came to you take over. You don't love me and you moved on. It was easy for you to forget what we had. But for me, Beulah, it hasn't gotten easier. Nothing has changed for me. I think about you every damn day. Falling in love with you wasn't something that disappeared when you did. My biggest fucking fear is I am always going to love you."

I understood the pain in his eyes as he spoke. Loving someone you can't be with was life altering. Constant emptiness and sorrow followed you everywhere. Jasper didn't stop loving me when we found out we were cousins. I'd been so horrified that I'd been able to shut off most of my emotions with him. I missed him and worried about him. I had thought I loved him until I truly fell in love with Stone. Then I knew the difference. If Jasper had loved me the way I loved Stone, we both experienced the same brokenness.

"We're related, Jasper. We couldn't be. We never had a chance."

He nodded. The sadness still there on his face. "I know, Beulah. But my heart doesn't give a fuck. I wish to God it did."

Through all of this, everything he'd done, everything I had grown to hate him for, I hadn't considered how he felt about me. I had never considered he was hurting and unable to move on. My world had become Stone so quickly afterward I didn't share the same pain Jasper did. Facing Jasper now knowing how hard it was to leave Stone because of the situation, I felt sympathy for Jasper. I guess what we felt was mutual regret. I should have been more sympathetic. I had moved on and thought he should too. My actions had been different but equally as cold as some of his had been to Stone.

"I'm sorry." The words were inadequate but needed to be said.

"Me too," he replied. "For a lot of shit and pain I caused. But I'm here now. You need me. I want to be needed. I'm not here to win you over. I know our reality will always make that impossible. But let me help you. If not for my sake let me help you because Stone called me. He trusted me enough to call me. I don't know why he can't be here. I don't know why he was so damn desperate that he called me, but he did. Let me stay with you. Not because I traced your phone and tracked you down, but because he wants me here. He needs to know you're safe," he stopped and let out a sigh. "And I need to know your safe."

There were a lot of things I could say at this moment. I wanted to argue with him about why he needed to leave. I could fight with him and send him back to Manhattan. I knew Stone was facing a fight that involved his son. If Jasper staying here eased his concern for me and he could focus on Wills then I was the cruel one to refuse it.

"I was thinking of staying here. In Tallahassee. My next step was looking at apartments," I told him.

"Follow me to return the rental car I'm in and we will figure out where to go. But seriously, Beulah, Tallahassee? There are better options. This may be Florida but they're really country here."

I liked that. "I'm country," I replied.

He chuckled. "Maybe but the good ole boys here don't make me feel real damn safe about ever leaving you. Can we try a few more cosmopolitan areas?"

I had no idea what he meant by that but I wasn't set on Tallahassee. I shrugged. "Sure. The only stipulation is I can't be too far away from Heidi."

"We don't have to go any further west. It's time we turned

north. You're in the deep south and moving further in. Time to run while you can."

I liked the idea of the deep south. But then what did I know?

Chapter Twenty-Nine
JASPER

KEEPING MY HEAD straight was going to be a challenge. When I was tracking her down it was easier to focus on doing it for Stone. Did I hate that he had her love? Yes, but since I ended our friendship with my dick move I realized I didn't hate him. He had the woman I wanted. The only woman I had ever wanted completely. But I didn't hate him. I missed him. When I needed advice, I'd catch myself thinking I'd call Stone. He always had an answer. I couldn't call him and that had hurt. It was a different hurt than losing Beulah, but just as powerful.

This had been my way to fix it. I had to fix what I'd lost with the best friend I'd ever had. However, once she walked out of the fast food place carrying that bag of food and her eyes locked on me, I felt it. The pull to her. Why couldn't I move on and let her go? She was right in the beginning. We couldn't ever be together. Not just because we were fucking related. But because of the twisted shit my parents had done. That darkness would always be there between us.

When I glanced over at her sitting there in the passenger seat asleep, it was hard to remember all of that. In the silence of her car, all I could remember was how it felt to hold her. How her smile fixed all the bad shit. And the way it felt to make love to her. Knowing what it felt like to be inside her was the hardest thing to forget. I doubted I ever would. I feared that I would only see her when I was inside someone else. That I wouldn't be able to truly give myself to anyone else.

I expected her to stay with Stone. I thought they'd be a forever thing. He was the kind of person you knew you could trust. He was solid. He was honest. And he loved her the way I did. Why she had run I didn't know. He hadn't told me and I wasn't real convinced he knew. There had to be a pretty damn big secret. Beulah wasn't one to run because of a misunderstanding. She'd need a reason. A real one.

She yawned and stretched which caught my attention again. I shifted my eyes to watch her briefly before looking back at the road in front of me. It wasn't that she was beautiful. I'd been with many beautiful women. It was more that her beauty. Something deeper and pure that couldn't be faked. It was there drawing you in. Making you want to be worthy of her.

"Where are we?" she asked with a raspy voice.

"An hour from Macon," I replied.

"Georgia!" she asked sitting up quickly.

"Yes, I did say we were going north," I reminded her. North of Tallahassee was Georgia.

"But I need to get out of the state. At least. It's why I went south. Florida was close but it was still a distance from Savannah." She sounded panicked. I wanted to know why she needed to leave

Savannah. What was it that was making her do this? I knew Stone wasn't a threat. There had to be something else.

"I was thinking Tennessee, but if that's too far we can go east and head into South Carolina. Not far but a different state," I told her.

She groaned. "This is using too much gas. I am on a budget. We can't keep driving all over the Southeast. I need to make a decision and go there."

I glanced at the gas tank. I'd filled it up an hour ago. "I'm paying for the gas while I'm with you," I told her. "Don't argue with me. I made the road trip longer than you intended for it to be. The gas is on me."

She lifted the side of her mouth in a smirk but she didn't argue. She was worried about money. Again, why would she leave a job she seemed to love and the security of Stone's apartment? What was it that would send her running? I started to ask and stopped myself. She wasn't going to tell me, it was pointless to pry.

"Hungry?" I asked. It was four hours since her breakfast and that hadn't been much. I'd expected her to pull out a chicken biscuit. That was what that place was famous for. But she'd had grilled nuggets and apples. Not exactly filling.

She nodded. "Yes."

I started looking for an exit with good food. Or at least decent food. There wasn't going to be that many options on this stretch of interstate. Not until we got closer to a large city. "What are you in the mood for?" I asked.

She shrugged. "Anything. I'm not picky."

I already knew that, but I hated to be the one to choose.

"Mexican?" I asked.

She didn't say anything and I glanced at her and she was

biting her bottom lip. I thought she liked Mexican but the strange nervous expression she was making made me think she'd changed her mind.

"Maybe not Mexican then. How about Italian? Pasta sound good?" I asked glancing back at her again to see her reaction.

She looked relieved and let go of the lip she was chewing on. "That sounds nice," she replied. I didn't ask what about Mexican set her off but it was going to bug me.

"I think there's an Italian place up ahead. I saw the sign for it a few miles back. They've got good breadsticks. Haven't been there in years though. Since my early college days."

She didn't say anything. I had texted Stone while I was getting gas and let him know I had found her and we were headed north from Tallahassee. I wasn't ready to be his buddy again. I had to work through my own shit and accept this. What I was doing and why. Then I could face him and apologize. Try to save a friendship I never thought I would be without.

He had simply texted. "Thank you." Nothing more. No questions. Honestly, his nonchalance had pissed me off. Did he not want to know how she was? If she was upset? Sad? Hurt? Anything? Fuck, he was a good man. I knew that. But when he shut you out he did it completely. Was he planning on doing that to her? Could he? And if he did would I be able to choose between the two?

I glanced at her side profile. She was alone in this world. I didn't know details but I knew she wasn't leaving Savannah easily. Heidi was too important to her. There had to be a very good reason. And I didn't believe it was her fault. Stone was the one who I knew could be so damn dark that it was hard to be around him. He could shut off and withdraw. It was easier to believe he had made a mistake. He had made her believe she wasn't wanted.

Than to think she had done anything to cause this.

His friendship was something I needed in this life. I knew that now better than I had before. Being without it hadn't been easy. But loving Beulah was the same. Being without her wasn't easy. If I eventually had to pick one it would be the hardest choice of my life.

"Jasper," she said almost too quietly.

"Yes?"

"I need you to pull over. Now." There was panic in her voice. I put on a blinker and slowed down to ease off the road. It wasn't safe to be on the side of the interstate, but I didn't question her. The moment I got the car stopped she threw open her door, jumped out and immediately bent at the waist and began to vomit. Over and over.

I watched her a second before it sank in. It began to make sense. Reaching for the door handle I got out of the car and walked around to her. The circumstances for her running, the sadness, the easy acceptance of my presence. It was all because of this.

When she was done, she put her hands on her knees and lifted her head to look at me. She was pale. Her eyes seemed larger than normal and they were now watery. "Thanks," she said then stood up. She didn't say more only turned went back to the car, got a napkin out of the bag from earlier, cleaned her face, put the napkin back in the bag and turned to place it on the ground outside. When she did she glanced back at me again. "I know it's littering but I can't . . . I need it out of the car."

The smell of the chicken. Vomiting after the mention of Mexican food. I had never personally spent time with a pregnant woman but I had seen enough television and movies. Stone had no idea. If he did, whatever he was doing right now that was so important he called me to come after her, would be dropped. He'd be here with her. Doing whatever he could to get her to come back.

She got in the car and closed the door. Walking back around to get back in myself I knew I was going to have to tell him. He deserved to know. She needed him to know. But before I did she was going to answer some questions. I wasn't going to shoot off at the mouth again with information I didn't have facts on. I was going to be more careful this time.

Starting the car, I pulled back onto the interstate. I didn't say anything. I let her sit there and think. She had to know I wasn't a complete idiot. What had just happened wasn't food poisoning or a stomach virus. If it were it would have been worse. She would be hunched over in the seat weak and sick.

The Italian place appeared the next exit sign and although I wasn't positive she could eat just yet I took the exit anyway. Our silence continued until I was parked and we were sitting there staring straight ahead. Both of us waiting for the other to speak. I wanted her to tell me. I didn't want to be the one to hammer her with questions, but I would if I had to.

"He doesn't want kids. He said him having a child would be a mistake." Her voice was so soft I had to strain to hear her.

Stone thought he should never be a father. He'd said more than once that he wouldn't know the first thing about it. He had no example to follow. All he had was Gerry and that wasn't enough, or so he believed.

"But he said that not knowing about you," I said making sure I understood correctly. Because if he knew she was carrying his child and he had said that fuck fixing our friendship. I'd find him and beat his ass or go down trying. Truth had always been Stone was the more dangerous one. He'd been fighting since he was young. That was the one thing his abusive father had taught him. Tough, hard, and cold. But he could also be the best human you'd ever met. It was a unique combination.

"I couldn't tell him. Not after that. I don't want my baby to ever feel like it was a mistake. Or unwanted. And if he feels that way our child will feel it too."

She spoke as if each word physically hurt her. She wouldn't look at me. I could see her chin quiver as she fought to hold in her emotion. When Stone found out I doubted he would ever forgive himself.

"I understand. But I also know Stone. He often says what he thinks and doesn't consider how it could change if the situation presented itself. I know he loves you. I understand that more than anyone else. And because I know how he feels and the sacrifice he was willing to make to secure your safety by calling me, I also know you're wrong about how he will feel about the baby."

If he didn't forgive me for anything else, what I'd just said should cleanse me from all the other sins I'd committed against him. Beulah was so vulnerable right now. I could take advantage of that and give her a life she didn't think she would have now. I could step in to be a father to the baby. She'd eventually love me. I could see that scenario and I would be a liar if I didn't admit it was tempting. But it was also wrong.

I knew the baby's father. I knew the truth. And I knew he would want her and this baby. She wasn't an abandoned single mother who needed me to save her. If she was, I'd gladly do it and thank God for a second chance. But this wasn't my lucky moment. It wasn't meant to be for us.

"Can you eat?" I asked her instead of pushing or trying to convince her on anything more.

She turned to look at me. A small sad smile touched her lips. "Actually, I'm craving those breadsticks you mentioned."

For now, I'd feed her. When she slept again I would decide what to do and how to handle it. Stone's future depended on it and this time I wasn't going to let him down.

Chapter Thirty
BEULAH

SOMEHOW I HAD managed to eat three breadsticks and an entire bowl of ravioli. When I had gotten sick for the first time I wasn't sure I could ever eat again. If it wasn't chicken or Mexican, it seemed I was fine in the hunger and eating department. The restaurant was more expensive than my budget. Jasper had threatened to make a scene if I didn't allow him to pay for the meal. When I tried to order salad and breadsticks only, he ordered me ravioli, lasagna and fettuccini alfredo. I had to promise to eat the ravioli to stop him from ordering everything else on the menu.

Over lunch he didn't mention Stone, the pregnancy, or what he thought I should do next. Instead, he told me funny stories about college. The story about Sterling when he had been locked out of the house without clothes and had to run naked to the neighbors to ask to use their phone had almost made me pee my pants. The neighbors had been in their late seventies and called the police on him. He'd run and hid in the woods, staying there all night until someone woke up in the house and finally let him inside.

I didn't completely forget my problems. But for a short moment I laughed and enjoyed the distraction. Once we were back in the car, my sorrow returned. I closed my eyes and sleep came easily. At least that was something I didn't have to worry about. My body was going to rest even if my mind wasn't cooperating.

When I woke again the trees were different. They weren't as green. It was almost as if fall was close and it wasn't the end of August. I sat up and looked around. "Where are we?" I knew this wasn't Georgia. With a quick glance at the clock on the dash I realized I'd been asleep for four hours.

"Somewhere in South Carolina," he replied with a smile. As if that answer was sufficient.

"Where in South Carolina?" I pressed.

"Not really sure. Haven't seen a sign in a while. Halfway through I'd guess."

"Halfway through? What's our the destination? I thought we were going to stop somewhere in this state."

He shrugged. "I figured since you weren't set on anything yet we'd look at North Carolina. See what you thought of it. We have time. This adventure is on me until I leave you where you finally decide."

Frustrated, I grabbed my phone to see if I could figure out where we were and how far from Savannah we were. There had to be a city around here that would be a good fit. "North Carolina is too far," I snapped.

"Didn't say you had to settle down there. Just thought we'd check it out."

"Ugh!" I groaned. "I need to find a job, Jasper. A place to

live. I don't have time to ride around and explore. Neither do you. You've got a corporation to run."

"It's fine for now. It's a phone call away. Besides it's getting late. You should get out and stretch your legs. Let's find a place to stop for the night."

I threw my hands up. "I have been sleeping at rest areas to save money. We aren't both fitting in this car tonight comfortably and you aren't paying for a hotel room. I've wasted a day when I should have been finding a home."

Tears burned my eyes as the frustration grew. I shouldn't have slept all day. This was my fault. I was messing it all up and I needed to focus.

"You slept in your car? In a rest area?" he asked me.

"Yes! It's free!"

"Jesus," he muttered something else under his breath but I didn't understand him nor did I care. I wasn't helpless. I was smart about it.

"I know where we can stop tonight. Tomorrow I'll let you guide me. I promise. But tonight, you're sleeping in a bed in a fucking hotel. Do it for my safety if not for yours. Because if Stone ever found out I allowed you to sleep in this car he'd murder me with his hands."

I doubted that but I also knew Jasper wasn't going to let up on this. I was sure he had never slept in a car in his life. I didn't imagine he would start tonight. No matter how much I demanded.

"Fine. But tomorrow this ends. I find a town and I stay there. You get on a plane back to Manhattan and live your life. Forget what you know and trust my decisions." Even as I said it I wondered if he would. There was a chance he'd tell Stone. Then I would be faced with that. Stone's decision wasn't going to change mine.

"I'll do whatever you say," he replied.

I had a hard time believing that. But I had to trust him and let him take us to a hotel. The day was almost over. And he was right, I wanted to get out and walk around. My legs ached from being in the car most of the day.

A sign up ahead said Beaufort. I'd heard of Beaufort. That was too close to Savannah. What was he doing? This wasn't my idea of distance. "Why are we so close to Savannah. This is not the way to North Carolina," I said stating the obvious. He hadn't been taking us toward North Carolina.

He shrugged. "I thought we'd drive up the coast."

More wasted time and gas. The coast was too expensive. I knew that already. I needed a small town away from the water. I shouldn't have slept. I should have been making plans. And getting mad at him was unfair.

"They've got some decent hotels here," he said as if that made it all better.

"Yes, hotels that will cost a fortune."

He frowned. "Not really. It's the river not the actual coast here."

I just rolled my eyes. Jasper would think anything less than a five star was average. It was his world and I never belonged in it to begin with.

I stayed silent as he chose a hotel that wasn't on the water but it wasn't cheap either. When he pulled up to the front, he turned to face me. "They'll get your bag." I wanted to grab my beat-up duffel bag and haul it inside with me but I got out and managed to smile at the man holding my door open before heading in the building.

Angry and worked up, I stayed sulking while Jasper checked us into the hotel. He brought me a room key. "Try and get some rest," he paused and his eyes seemed almost as if he were asking for forgiveness. "I only want to help. That was my goal. To make up for all the harm I had caused."

I felt bad for being so difficult. He had been nothing but nice and patient with me. If I was honest, not being alone had made this easier. He wasn't trying to upset me. This was just his way of doing things. "Thank you. You've been great today. I'm just . . . I've got a lot on my mind and I don't mean to be so testy."

He smiled. "It will be okay."

One day maybe it would be—it wouldn't be for a while. I didn't say that though. I simply nodded. "Goodnight," I said instead.

"Goodnight, Beulah." The way he said my name sounded like it meant more. There was something in his tone that struck me. I paused and studied him a moment. Then figured I was reading too much into it. I was emotionally raw these days.

With one last smile, I left him there and went to find my room.

Chapter Thirty-One
STONE

I STOOD OUTSIDE the hotel in Beaufort, South Carolina that Jasper had said he'd take her to. When he called me earlier today I hadn't wanted to answer his call. My father had just sent word from his lawyer to mine that if I continued the course of action I was taking that I would regret it.

He knew I was going to fight for Wills. That was why he'd sent him away. Wills wasn't at a boarding school, I had found that out quickly enough. He was staying in my father's newest house in London. The boarding school had been a smoke screen.

I answered the call because Jasper was with Beulah. I hadn't expected him to call me when he was with her. I fully expected him to take advantage of the situation to try and win her back. That was the reason I answered.

I greeted him by saying I didn't have time for his bullshit. If he couldn't take care of her I'd send someone else. What he said next, however, had brought me here.

"Sending someone else to take care of the woman carrying your child that she believes you don't fucking want—and I believe you called a mistake—would be the biggest jackass move of your life."

I had stood there frozen in shock. It had taken him saying. "Do you hear me you cold motherfucker? She's pregnant. She's not run from you. She left to protect her baby that she thinks you can't love. That's what I am dealing with here. I had to pull over while she vomited on the side of the interstate. I had to force her to let me pay for her meal so she'd eat more than a damn salad and I had to threaten her with you to get her to let me put her up in a hotel tonight. Because she's slept in her CAR in a fucking REST AREA for the past two nights. Is this all sinking in?"

Fear and panic didn't begin to describe what I was feeling. "Where is she?" I asked.

"I'll text you the location of the hotel I am taking her to. If you don't show up, I'll step in. I'll be what she needs and in time she'll love me again. This is my peace offering. Come get her if she and your baby are what you want. If you think you can't be a father then let me be one. I had a shit example too, but because of it I know what not to do. And so the fuck do you."

He promptly ended the call.

And I ordered a private plane without contacting my lawyers, without thinking about my next steps with my father—that would have to wait. Finding Beulah and getting her home wouldn't. I had to save my future.

During the flight here, I'd replayed all the words I'd said that last night we'd been together. I remembered how I had gone on and on about us not having a baby. How getting her pregnant would be a mistake I didn't want. Each fucking memory was like a knife stabbing me in the chest. To think she had stood there and listened to me knowing our child was already growing inside her. I was so ashamed of myself.

How did she not completely break apart right there? How had she stood so damn strong and held it together? Any other woman would have thrown something at my head and cursed me for the bastard I was.

I texted Jasper. "I am here. What room number?"

He didn't respond and I stood there waiting. Just when I was ready to walk inside and demand to know where she was, Jasper appeared. He walked out the front entrance and came toward me. A scowl of determination on his face.

"What I did before, it was wrong. I was hurt, bitter, and I was desperate to win her back. But I lost something else. Something I hadn't realized that was more important—my best friend. The only real family I have. This," he said pointing back at the hotel. "This is me asking for forgiveness. I was tempted to keep her secret. To be the man she needed. To be the hero. But I couldn't."

His apology was unexpected. That wasn't what I had thought he'd come out here to say. Jasper was the one person I knew about as well as I knew myself. We were different but we'd both lived similar childhoods. We had made it through tough times depending on the other one.

"You left something out," I said.

He frowned but didn't ask what.

"You called me because you love her. It wasn't all about me. Or us. It was about her too. You chose what you knew she wanted instead of what you wanted."

He chuckled softly but there was no humor there. "Maybe so."

I held out my hand and he looked at it then placed his in

mine. We shook then he stepped forward and hugged me. After a slap on the back he stepped back.

"Room 202. Here's the extra key I had them make. Go fix your fucking disaster. And next time think before you go rambling off at the mouth."

I took the key. "Thanks," I said.

Jasper nodded, turned and walked toward the parking lot.

"Where are you going?" I asked knowing he had no car here.

"I had a rental sent here after I called you. I knew you'd show up and I want to continue my road trip."

I watched him walk away before heading inside. We weren't what we had once been but we were mending. One day I knew we would have that again. It would be when I knew he wasn't looking at my wife wanting her. He'd have to find his own happiness first. I was only so understanding.

Heading to the entrance, I held the key in my hand and my steps grew longer and swifter. The need to see her clawed at me. I wanted to hold her and reassure myself she was safe. The elevator was empty since it was the middle of the night and I was outside her door within minutes.

Taking the key, I tapped the lock and was relieved when the red light didn't flash because she had bolted it. Knocking on her door would have been more difficult. There was a good chance if the lock had been engaged that she wouldn't wake up and I'd have to sit out here until morning to see her.

Stepping into the dark room, I closed the door quietly behind me. I turned on the bathroom light and cracked the door to give me some visibility. She needed to see my face when she opened her eyes so she didn't think a stranger was in here with her.

She was curled up in the middle of a king size bed. I could

see her pink pajamas peeking through the little bit of her that wasn't covered up. She seemed so fragile to me now. I wanted to carry her around in bubble wrap and keep her safe from the world. Keep them both safe.

I sat down on the edge of the bed and reached over to touch her arm. Letting her sleep would come later. I couldn't allow any more time to pass with her believing I didn't want our child. Even in her dreams she needed to know the truth.

Her eyes fluttered open and she gasped. She started to sit up when her eyes locked on me. She froze and stared at me as if she wasn't sure I was real. She blinked again and rubbed her eyes and stared at me harder. Squinting to see if I was still there. It as adorable but it also broke my heart. To think she would believe I wouldn't love our child. That the stupid words I'd said while upset about Wills would mean anything more than an emotional man's rant.

"Am I awake?" she whispered.

"Yes," I assured her.

She sat there thinking about it a moment more. I let her slowly take everything in.

"Jasper told you?" she said the words as if they were a question more than a statement.

"He did."

She frowned. "What did he tell you?"

"That I was a bastard that needed to think before I spoke." She didn't stop frowning. She was being careful. I realized she was protecting our baby. Although I deserved it her distrust of me was like a punch in the gut. "He also told me that my future, my happiness, and the woman I loved were in Beaufort, South Carolina and she was carrying my child." I reached out and cupped her face with my hand. "I'm sorry, Beulah. For saying what I did. I was upset about Wills. I was saying shit without thinking. Things I didn't mean."

She looked at me nervously. "I can't . . . I can't let my baby ever feel as if it wasn't wanted. I, I love you. I will always love you. But if you can't be a father. If this is too much, please leave. Don't force something you don't want. It will cause harm I can never fix."

Leaning down so that our faces were only inches apart I made sure she could see my eyes clearly. I never wanted her to doubt what I was saying. My soul was bared. "I want you and our baby more than I want my next breath. I was scared I couldn't be a father. But someone smarter than I gave him credit for pointed out that I knew exactly what not to do. That I knew what a kid needed because I never had it. I also know that a child created from the love I have for you will be impossible not to love. I want you, I want our child, and I want you. Forever. I have since the beginning and that will never change."

Tears filled her eyes and she reached up to cover my hand with hers. "Let's go home."

The word home meant so many things to me over my life. But never had they meant happiness. With Beulah I realized that although we would face hard times and our lives wouldn't always be perfect, we had each other. She would be my home. And so would our children. The child she was carrying and the one I would fight for until he was with us.

Epilogue

DARK BROWN CURLS danced in the wind as laughter carried across the field. I smiled as I drank my tea on the back porch of our home. I loved hearing their laughter. It never failed to bring a smile to my face. Prim tilted her head back to look up at her big brother as he pushed her on the swing set she'd gotten for her third birthday last week.

Wills was her hero. From the moment she could toddle around on two feet, she'd been following Wills around the house. When he left for school she would stand at the door with big crocodile tears in her eyes watching him go. The moment he walked in the door in the afternoon, she would run to him with her arms wide open.

There was a time I feared she may not get to know her brother. That he'd forever be kept from her. Stone had gone after his father with everything he had. Child abuse had been his first accusation. Not just for Wills but the abuse he had suffered. Then he'd submitted the proof of Wills' DNA.

The trial never came and the fight ended quickly. Not because his father backed down but because he suffered a stroke that put him in a coma for six months. During that time Stone was able to get temporary custody of Wills. Having him with us had been wonderful but we still were haunted that it might prove temporary. Now that we had Wills, losing him wasn't something neither of us could face. Stone worked hard to continue to build a case against his father. Hilda was unresponsive to any contact we attempted with her. She didn't want to lose the life she now had in Malibu.

When his father didn't wake from the coma but his body started slipping away, Stone was called in because his current stepmother wasn't on his living will as the person to make the decision to pull him off life support. Stone was. He couldn't make the call that day. It was something he had to be sure was the right thing to do. He spoke with several doctors. Each one said his father was slowly passing and there was less and less brain activity. To the point if he ever woke up he'd be in a vegetative state at best.

Stone didn't sleep that night. He'd sat outside on the porch.

He made the final decision, and one week before I gave birth to our daughter, Stone's father was buried. His stepmother didn't contest the will seeing as she received the home in Manhattan and twenty-million dollars. Much more than she would have gotten in a divorce. The prenup made that very clear.

Hilda once again signed over custody of her child. This time to Stone when the courts tried to say that Wills legally went to his mother. Wills didn't even ask to see his mother. He began to accept that he was safe with us. That we loved him and he had a home here. Soon he began to act more like the child he was than the child too old for his years.

Heidi loved coming to stay with us over the weekends and spending holidays together. She adored her niece and nephew, and they loved her. She had a room in our home if she ever wanted to live with us, but she was happy with her life at Among the Spanish Moss.

The door behind me opened and I turned to see my handsome husband walk outside. He was watching the kids play with a pleased smile. His eyes shifted to me. "How you feeling?" he asked.

I held up my cup. "The ginger tea Geraldine suggested works well. Wish I'd known when I was sick with Prim."

Stone walked over and pressed a kiss to my head. "You decided when we're gonna tell them yet?" he asked referring to the kids.

I hadn't yet so I shook my head.

He shrugged. "Whenever you're ready. No hurry. We can let them think you're getting fat."

I shoved him and laughed. "Not funny," I said not amused even a little.

"I like it when you're big and round. It's the only time I know Jasper isn't looking at my wife and imagining her naked."

"He doesn't do that," I replied then rolled my eyes.

"Hell yeah, he does."

The kids loved their Uncle Jasper and I was thankful the relationship between Stone and Jasper had been restored. They needed each other. They weren't brothers by blood, but they were brothers in every way that mattered.

Stone sat on the couch beside me and pulled me into his lap. "Come here. I need to hold you before you get too heavy."

"If I didn't love you, I'd hate you," I told him.

"You couldn't hate me. I'm too damn lovable."

He was right, he was. At one time, he didn't believe that.

At one time, I didn't believe it either. But life has a funny way of playing out in ways you never imagined.

A boy walked into my world one day and I thought he was the most rude, beautiful, unlikable person I'd ever met. And now I couldn't imagine a day without him by my side.

Acknowledgements

THIS STORY HAS been one more ride. From the moment Beulah and Stone's story came to me until I wrote the last sentence in the epilogue. I always love telling a story. This one was special. Just like a reader wants to find a moment to get lost in a book, I looked forward to the times I would sit at my computer and their story would unfold for me. It was a beautiful tale that will remain one of my favorites.

There are so many people that played a part in this trilogy's creation, production and promotion.

The first person that reads what I write (and holds me accountable for word count on a daily basis) is Britt. Jack Britton Sullivan, my youngest child's father, reads my words every morning when he wakes up. He not only helps me mold the story he also gives me ideas when I get stuck or unsure. This kind of support is priceless.

Next there is Amy Donnelly who works with my crazy unorganized last minute ways. She takes what I hand her and turns it around in record time to make it exactly what I wanted it to look like.

Christine Borgford also is a complete life saver. Her formatting is beautiful and she deals with my last minute requests and rushed deadlines. Never complaining and always giving me an amazing product.

This trilogy would not exist if Ian Wallace from iBooks hadn't contacted me about writing iBooks an exclusive trilogy. The entire team at iBooks is incredible. They are there for support whenever I need them. I've loved every moment of this experience with them. Thank you iBooks!

Hang Le for the beautiful covers. Each one fits the story perfectly. She was a pleasure to work with. I couldn't be happier with the cover art for each book.

Danielle Lagasse, Vicci Kaighan and the rest of Abbi's Army. These ladies are my ultimate support group. They amaze me daily. I love you all!

Kiki Chatfield who is incredible at what she does. Her marketing, organization and enthusiasm has helped get the Sweet Series in front of so many new readers.

Colleen Hoover and Kami Garcia for taking the time out of their incredibly busy lives to read and blurb Sweet Little Thing. Friends like them are hard to find. I'm truly grateful.

Monica Tucker- the world's most patient personal assistant (aka life handler) on the planet. You have no idea how hard I am to get things from. I forget, I'm ADD, I am a hot mess. And she deals with it beautifully.

My kids- Austin, Annabelle, Ava and Emerson- who without them I would have no reason to do any of this. They inspire me, bring me joy, and complete my world. I love y'all.

ABBI GLINES

ABBI GLINES IS a #1 New York Times, USA Today, and Wall Street Journal bestselling author of the Rosemary Beach, Sea Breeze, Vincent Boys, Existence, and The Field Party Series. She never cooks unless baking during the Christmas holiday counts. She believes in ghosts and has a habit of asking people if their house is haunted before she goes in it. She drinks afternoon tea because she wants to be British but alas she was born in Alabama. When asked how many books she has written she has to stop and count on her fingers. When she's not locked away writing, she is reading, shopping (major shoe and purse addiction), sneaking off to the movies alone, and listening to the drama in her teenagers lives while making mental notes on the good stuff to use later. Don't judge.

You can connect with Abbi online in several different ways. She uses social media to procrastinate.

www.abbiglines.com
www.facebook.com/abbiglinesauthor
twitter.com/AbbiGlines
www.instagram.com/abbiglines
www.pinterest.com/abbiglines

books by
ABBI GLINES

As She Fades

ROSEMARY BEACH SERIES
Fallen Too Far
Never Too Far
Forever Too Far
Rush Too Far
Twisted Perfection
Simple Perfection
Take A Chance
One More Chance
You We're Mine
Kiro's Emily
When I'm Gone
When You're Back
The Best Goodbye
Up In Flames

SEA BREEZE SERIES
Breathe
Because of Low
While It Lasts
Just For Now
Sometimes It Lasts
Misbehaving
Bad For You
Hold On Tight
Until The End

SEA BREEZE MEETS ROSEMARY BEACH
Like A Memory
Because of Lila

THE FIELD PARTY SERIES
Until Friday Night
Under the Lights
After the Game

ONCE SHE DREAMED
Once She Dreamed (Part 1)
Once She Dreamed (Part 2)

THE VINCENT BOYS SERIES
The Vincent Boys
The Vincent Brothers

THE MASON DIXON SERIES
Boys South of the Mason Dixon
Brothers South of the Mason Dixon

THE SWEET SERIES
Sweet Little Thing
Sweet Little Lies
Sweet Little Memories

EXISTENCE TRILOGY
Existence (Book 1)
Predestined (Book 2)
Leif (Book 2.5)
Ceaseless (Book 3)

Made in the USA
Lexington, KY
13 June 2018